Verity Wheelwright lives a life of luxury but boredom. She is the only daughter to the widowed Lord Wheelwright, and he keeps her in his manor on New Lutetia, where she meets with tutors to learn classical literature and music. Verity craves adventure and often escapes to the pages of livre rouge—cheap, paperback books with crimson covers that contain sordid tales of lust and adventure. When New Lutetia is invaded by the infamous airship pirate Cavalier Eli Callahan, Verity is forced to make a choice. She can run and hide, or surrender herself in exchange for the safety of her city, but at what cost?

The Airship Pirate
Copyright © 2021 Minerva Pendleton
ISBN: 978-1-4874-3262-1
Cover art by Martine Jardin

Published by eXtasy Books Inc or
Devine Destinies, an imprint of eXtasy Books Inc

Look for us online at:
www.eXtasybooks.com or www.devinedestinies.com

THE AIRSHIP PIRATE

BY

MINERVA PENDLETON

CHAPTER ONE: LIVRE ROUGE

"Oh, Miss Verity. Lord Wheelwright wouldn't want you reading something like that!"

Verity stopped rocking in her chair and looked over the top of her book at her maid. "No, Prudence. My father wouldn't like me reading much of anything that he or my tutors haven't personally selected and approved, and certainly nothing like this. Which is why you won't be telling him upon his return, will you?"

"Now Miss Verity," Prudence said, blushing slightly, "you know I'm under orders. If the master asks something . . ."

"Yes," Verity interrupted Prudence's oft-practiced speech, "I know very well about your orders. You are, however, my maid, and while you may be in my father's employ, you are directly beholden to me. Therefore, it would behoove you to keep a stealthy tongue about such matters."

"But Miss, if he knew you'd been shopping the stalls in Cocotte . . ."

Verity closed her book and place it in her lap. "Prudence, you know very well that I would not stoop to visiting Cocotte or any of the environs around the air docks. I simply paid for a slight favor from the hall boy on his day off."

"But Miss, a livre rouge . . ."

"Prudence, you cannot, as they say, judge a book by its cover. While this may be a poorly crafted book, made of cheap red cardstock and even cheaper paper, for all you know it may be a ring of sonnets from Boudicia or a series of lyric odes from ancient Hellenia."

Prudence bustled around the room, checking the levels on the warming engine in the corner, making sure the room was comfortable enough for sleep. "Yes, Miss," she said, turning to the bed to make sure Verity's night clothes were laid out properly for the evening, "only I know that your father's library has all the known translations from Hellenia and most of the classical poetry from Boudicia. Furthermore, I know that you could afford a much better-crafted book on practically any subject at a respectable book merchant in Colline Riche, like Seth and Wilf's or Chelonian Mobile. Any subject, I say, because I happen to know that my brother will occasionally pick up books similar to the one you're holding for our nan and read them to her while they split a fifth of Geneva liquor between them. Such tales are rarely fit for the eyes of a lady such as yourself, Miss."

"Well, I find such tales quite historical and educational," Verity said, settling back into the chair.

"Do you, Miss? Then, may I ask, what tale it is that you're reading? Just so I know what not to tell his lordship when he enquires about your independent studies."

"If you must know, I am enjoying a historical novel."

"And its title, Miss?"

Now it was Verity's turn to blush. "Devil Tooth Norton and the Bride of Encornet."

"Miss! An air pirate novel. Set in Encornet? I knew the book would be in poor taste, but surely you see nothing of value in such . . . smut!"

Verity closed the book with her thumb marking her page and placed it in her lap. "It happens that I do, dear Prudence. First, I find the anatomical descriptions quite educational. My tutors have been quite mum on such subjects, and while I am versed in both Boudician and Clovisian literature, along with various classical texts, mathematics, and even musicianship, I am kept far away from the sciences, certainly those of human anatomy. Furthermore, while my father expects me to be a bride one day, helping to expand his qunubu plantation empire and provide him grandchildren to whom he will bequeath his lands and titles, he is rather remiss in explaining the particulars of human conception and reproduction."

Prudence blushed. "Well, yes, Miss. Normally your mother . . ."

"Yes, Prudence. Normally my mother would provide me with such instruction, or an aunt. But seeing as my mother passed away giving birth to me, and both she and my father are without siblings, and seeing as my tutors avoid the subject at all cost, I am left to my own learning. A few liard to the hall boy to sneak off to the stalls of Cocotte is surely a sound investment if I am to learn anything about being a woman."

Avoiding direct eye contact, Prudence busied herself by poking the coals in Verity's fireplace, warming up the room slightly. "But Miss, I doubt any tales set in Encornet will teach you the virtues of being a woman."

"Yes, Prudence," Verity sighed, "it is true that the women of Encornet, at least the ones in this tome, are certainly soiled doves who have traded what few virtues they have for money and drink. However, from my understanding of marriage, a bride is nothing more than a harlot with a much more extravagant price tag that her husband pays to her father. A lady in Encornet may trade away her virtue for a few coins, while a bride may trade away hers for land and title, but ultimately the act of congress must be the same. I can't imagine the parts, or their machinations, work any differently simply because the price is higher. And if this author is to be believed, a lady may derive much pleasure from such engagements if she handles herself properly."

"Well, that may be true, Miss," Prudence said, pulling the bed covers back for Verity and fluffing her pillows slightly, "but I'm not sure your father would willingly wed you off to an airship pirate. Certainly not one like Devil Tooth Norton."

Verity laughed a bit too deliberately. "I have no intention of marrying an airship pirate, Prudence. And I'm sure I could never kiss a man nicknamed *Devil Tooth*, let alone marry one. No, I'm sure my father will set me up with some proper gentleman with copious land holdings on the New Continent, and I shall live out my life on some sweaty plantation producing babies and hosting tea parties for the ladies of the county.

"But just once, I'd like to meet a man who had more concerns in life than his pecuniary holdings. Can't you imagine being carried off on a ship like The Devil's Grog, tearing through the clouds while being pursued by gendarmes, escaping to some remote port to divvy up the plunder and waltz the night away with a man like Cavalier Eli Calahan?"

"Oh, Miss, now that's just stuff and nonsense. Everybody knows Eli Calahan is a storybook fabrication, and no airship pirate ever acted like that. They're all just lowly thieves and barbarians, common murderers and criminals barely fit to be called human. Now, it's time for you to retire. Come now, into bed with you."

"But think about the adventure, Prudence," sighed Verity as she stood and made her way to the bed, placing the book on the nightstand beside the gas lamp, "the honor of being with a gentleman like that."

"If there ever were a gentleman like that, I'd say he'd have better things to do with his life than traipsing around the sky in an airship robbing the gentry of what's rightfully theirs. There's certainly no honor in stealing, nor in the murdering that goes along with it, if the stories are to be believed. Now, into your bedclothes."

Verity, with Prudence's help, squeezed herself out of her dress and pulled on her nightgown. Then she climbed into bed. "You're right, Prudence. For a change, I'd like to do something with my day besides practice arithmetic and eat a supper that the cook has ensured will enhance my figure without ruining my constitution. I may as well be a horse in my father's stable for all anyone is concerned, with enough money in the saddle bags to tempt a husband."

"Now, Miss, you know your father is only doing what's best for you. You've come of age, to be sure, and he simply wants what's best for his little girl."

"But I'm not a girl, Prudence. I'm nearly twenty-four, and I've seen nothing of the world but the city of New Lutetia and my father's plantation house in Bourbonia on the New Continent. A woman my age should be doing things with her life, not memorizing sums and learning entertaining nocturnes on the piano. I'm sure the ladies of Encornet have much more exciting lives."

"And I'm sure those ladies are stone dead by thirty, begging your pardon, Miss, and each and every one of them would give their eyeteeth to live one day in your life where they don't have to worry about where their next meal is coming from or where they'll be sleeping that night. Now, no more talk of harlots or airship pirates or any such nonsense. We'll not mention this," she said, holding up the red book to Verity, "to your father, but we'll have no more livre rouge in the house, or I'll have to speak up. I'll get rid of this for you, Miss, but you're putting me in a fierce compromise."

"I suppose you're right," said Verity as she slumped into her pillows. "Why don't you pass it on to your brother for your nan. At least someone will get some enjoyment from it. And I know you'll have words with the hall boy, but do be gentle. I did give him an order and swore him to the strictest of confidences."

"As you say, Miss," said Prudence with a nod as she pulled the blankets up to Verity's chin, then turned to dim the gas lamp. "I'll overlook his impropriety this time. Now, it's time for you to sleep. We'll speak no more of this, and I'll make sure his lordship doesn't hear about it. Good night, Miss."

"Thank you, Prudence," said Verity as her eyes slowly closed, "and good night."

CHAPTER TWO: DRAPEAU BLANC

Verity awoke to the echoing sound of thunder. A crimson light peeked between the curtains of her bedroom. "Pilots take warning," she mumbled as she turned over to go back to sleep. Surely she had a few more minutes of rest before Prudence and her retinue came in to dress her for breakfast.

Verity glanced at the clock on her wall before closing her eyes, then sat up quickly. The clock said it was almost two in the afternoon. Well past breakfast and luncheon. Even if Prudence had come down with some illness, one of the other maids would have stepped up to take over her duties and wake and dress Verity. Certainly, something was amiss.

Verity got out of bed and walked to her window. She pulled back the curtains and gasped.

New Lutetia, her city and the only home she had ever known, was in flames. From her window, thanks to the distant hill upon which her father's mansion was built, she could see over the western part of the town, kilometers all the way down to the air docks and the Cocotte neighborhood which served their crews. Every few seconds, a popping explosion punctuated the sky, an airship bursting into flames and crashing into the ground below. Black smoke billowed up from the wreckage. She could see pockets of flames throughout the city, places where the fire had taken hold already.

But something wasn't right. Even in her surprise and panic, Verity knew that if the fire began in the docks, it should have worked its way up through Cocotte to the surrounding areas, even if it made it through the barricades designed to protect against such emergencies. There was no way that the fire could spread so sporadically throughout the town if it was merely an industrial accident. Unless . . .

Then Verity saw it. Through the plumes of smoke and the billows sparks and flame that rose through the city, an airship lumbered forth. It was moving much more slowly than a traditional airship, and she could see the pointed bursts erupt from its hull as it rained down hellfire on New Lutetia. The craft moved in a patient, deliberate manner, clearly attempting to cause as much devastation as possible as it wound its way forward. But still it came on, steadily working its way over the town towards Wheelwright Manor, towards her.

As the ship turned, Verity almost shrieked in panic. Its balloon was an eerie sable cloth, even more threatening against a background of smoke and fire. Painted on the balloon in bright crimson was a bottle emblazoned with a horned skull.

"The Devil's Grog," whispered Verity under her breath.

Here, before her very eyes, a ship of pure legend and fantasy was baptizing her city in hellfire. She knew this was no dream. She could already smell the smoke from the town, the stench of burning wood and gunpowder. She could see the flames as they caught hold of more and more of the buildings. Even though she could not see them, she could feel the waves of panic rippling throughout the city, and almost hear the screams of the people as they tried to survive the onslaught. Through it all, The Devil's Grog churned forth, advancing slowly towards her.

The bedroom door burst open and Prudence came running in, followed by Andrew, the head of her father's guards.

"The city's under attack, Miss! You must hurry. They're already through Barye Gate and are heading towards Wheelwright Manor!"

"No," said Verity definitely, "I will not run."

"But Miss," gasped Prudence, "you're his lordship's daughter. They're coming for you. They'll ransom you."

"Yes," said Verity, turning around and heading towards her wardrobe, "I am my father's daughter. As my father is away negotiating business with Lord Chattoway, it is up to me to protect the city. We have limited arms, so someone must negotiate surrender. Come, help me get dressed."

"But Miss," Prudence began to plead.

"Silence." Verity's voice cut Prudence off with such a loud command that even she was shocked. Both Prudence and Andrew stared — Verity knew she'd never spoken to them with such force or command. She wasn't sure if it was the fear or panic speaking, but she knew this was her chance, and she wasn't going to pass it up. She mustered every ounce of her father's authority in her voice, speaking quickly and with determined aplomb.

"I know my father gave you orders, but my father is not here. In his stead, I am in charge of this household and its staff. So I am now giving you the orders, and we simply do not have time to waste. My duty is to the staff of this household and the people of this city. If I am to be kidnapped and held for ransom to protect those lives, so be it.

She lifted her chin proudly with every ounce of aristocratic bravery she could muster, then started barking commands which she punctuated with her finger. "You will help me get dressed. Then you and Andrew will gather the rest of the staff and take them out through the secret passage in the wine cellar to my father's private landing platform. The Fritillaria is docked there and has enough room for all of you. It will be tight, but you'll be safe. Captain Bustard will be there, tending to the ship. He can get you to safety, certainly to one of the forts on Vache Bay. From there, you will contact my father. Now hurry. I'm certainly not going to negotiate the town's surrender in my dressing gown."

Verity was prepared for a rebuttal from Prudence, and even half expected Andrew to heft her over his shoulder and carry her off to safety. But Prudence simply nodded and began searching the wardrobe for an appropriate dress while Andrew snapped off a smart salute and stood in the doorway, waiting.

"You'll be wanting the green velvet, Miss," Prudence said. "It'll be cold on an airship, and there's no telling what accommodations they'll give you." She pulled out the dress, a simple day dress with a minimal bustle, good for casual everyday wear.

"Yes, this will do. No sense in giving these bastards airs above their station, begging your pardon, Miss. Now, off with you, Andrew. Go gather the staff like her ladyship said."

Andrew nodded, and quickly ran out the room. Prudence turned back to Verity. "I love you like my daughter. You know that, Miss."

"I know," said Verity.

"Me and Andrew will look to the staff, and no mistake, Miss," said Prudence as she helped Verity out of her nightgown and into the velvet dress, "and we will get to your father as soon as possible. You take care of yourself, and always remember that you are a lady." She kissed Verity on her cheek. "I know you'll do what's right, Miss. Be safe."

"I'll need something white, Prudence."

"Take the bed sheet from the bottom drawer, Miss. It needs mending anyway."

Verity smiled, then grabbed Prudence up in a big hug. "Be safe. This will be all over soon, and I'll see you when I can."

"As you say, Miss," said Prudence, who curtsied, then turned and ran out the bedroom door.

Verity yanked open the bottom drawer of her wardrobe and grabbed the bed sheet. Then she looked around the room quickly, and saw the tapestry hanging from her wall. She lifted the display bar off its wall hooks and slid the tapestry off the pole. Then she ran out of her room to meet her adversaries.

Verity was used to seeing men, of course. She had grown up with her father and his friends, as well as the multitude of male serving staff in the manor. But rarely had she seen anyone as disheveled and filthy as the men who kicked in the front doors of the manor and came tumbling in. The first thing that hit Verity was the smell, a stench of unwashed bodies perfumed with a sweet alcoholic aroma and exotic spices which billowed off their bodies and nearly knocked Verity off the chair she was standing upon. She was shocked at how filthy and ragged these men were, some of them barely dressed beyond a pair of ragged trousers and cheap leather sandals. There were almost a dozen all together, each one a sneering, lecherous fiend with ragged teeth and leathered skin. The pistols and rapiers they held were quite real, though.

Verity wondered if her theatrics were enough to stay their immediate attack. She had tied the bed sheet to the pole of the tapestry display and held it aloft. She had also draped herself with the ceremonial flag of New Lutetia, which she had torn off the wall in her father's library. Standing on a chair in an effort to seem more imposing, she struck what she hoped was a regal and devastating figure, glaring at the intruders with every ounce of disdain she could muster. Hopefully, it would be enough to buy her some time to improvise.

"Well, well, what do we have here?" barked one of the men, a bandana-wearing brute who seemed to be leading the party. "A regular Jeanne Hachette, but without her edge. Aren't you a pretty thing? Do you know what we do with pretty things like you, mon canard?"

Verity puffed out her chest and bellowed in her most commanding voice, "I am Lady Verity Wheelwright, daughter and sole heir of Lord Victor Wheelwright, and executive representative for the city of New Lutetia. I demand arbitration in accordance with the laws of Hugo Grotius and come forth displaying the drapeau blanc as a tacit sign demanding such."

"Do you now," a voice in the back of the group chuckled, "and what's to stop us from sampling the goods before we filch you off to the ship for some sport?"

"Silence that tongue, Bug Face, or I'll slice it out of your head and wipe your shit-stained ass with it," shouted the man with the bandana, spinning around the face the group. "The lady carries the drapeau blanc. We will honor the drapeau blanc, and any man among you that even thinks about laying a finger upon her before the arbitration is settled best figure out really quick how you'll work the ship with my blade sticking out of your belly. So help me God, the lady has come forth for arbitration with the captain, and she shall have arbitration with the captain, and she'll do so without a fuss." He turned back to Verity and gave a slight bow. "M'lady, in your own time."

The pirates surrounded Verity as she gingerly stepped down from the chair. She kept her chin held high and her fist clenched around her impromptu flagpole. Clearly her plan had worked, so far. Whoever this man in the bandana was, he was obviously in charge and commanded the respect of the rest of the rabble. He also respected the laws of warfare, apparently, and she assumed it would behoove her to make friends with him. "May I enquire as to the identity of my escort, good sir?" she asked, trying to be as genteel as possible. The man in the bandana looked at her quizzically. "Your name, good sir?"

He nodded, understandingly. "Abraham Bloom, m'lady. But them that knows me calls me Screw." The rest of the pirates chuckled at this and were immediately silenced by a dagger look from Abraham's face.

Verity assumed that his nickname was sexual in nature and made a determined effort to look neither shocked nor affronted. "Well, then, Mr. Screw," she said, offering him her hand, "please escort me to your captain."

Abraham looked at her hand as though it were a cocked pistol pointed at him, then looked up at his companions, who seemed as daunted as he was. He shrugged and took it, leading Verity out of the broken doorway and down the gravel carriage way that led to the manor gates. In an effort to maintain some semblance of propriety, she removed her hand deftly from Abraham's and took him by the elbow, forcing him to walk more slowly as to keep pace with her shorter steps.

The absurdity of the situation only seemed to serve her purpose, as he was not used to escorting a lady, and stumbled and shuffled awkwardly. The tableau would have been a farce for anyone who might have seen it. Verity's green velvet day dress was a sharp contrast to this man's ragged linen shirt and patched canvas shorts, and her lavender-soaped and powdered skin was a pale elegance compared with his hairy, tanned hide. The bed sheet tied to the pole in her hand caught the night breeze and swelled like a sail, only adding to the preposterous image.

A small winged carriage waited outside the gate. The driver was hunched over the steering mechanism, staring at a pocket watch. "Took your time about it, didn't you, Screw."

"Button that gob, Chillum, and get ready to rendezvous with the Grog." Abraham turned and addressed the rest of his party. "We got what we came for, but there's plenty to be had, I'm sure. Get what you can and bring it back within the hour, or face the gendarmes and their irons."

A cheer went up from the group, and they scattered as Abraham helped Verity into the carriage, which was beginning to bounce under the pressure of the built-up steam.

"Don't worry, m'lady," he said as he climbed in after her, "these steam-powered muscas from Cathay give a bumpy ride, but they're safe enough. Chillum knows his business and no mistake. We'll get you to the captain in one piece." He nodded at the flag, which Verity still had clutched in her hand. "You can let go of that, too, if you'd be more comfortable. On my mother's grave, no one will lay a finger on you."

"I respect your departed mother, Mr. Screw," said Verity, almost yelping as the vehicle lurched into the air, "but I think I'll hold onto it just in case."

"Suit yourself," said Abraham, scratching at his bandana, "but the captain knows his history and maintains his honor. No one will harm you."

"I've read all about men like your captain, Mr. Screw," Verity snapped, "and I'm well aware of their definition of honor. I am also well aware of my predicament, and I only hope to serve my people, even at the cost of my own virtue and personal safety."

Abraham started to laugh. "Well, m'lady, I'm sure your research and expertise will be quite useful to your negotiations. There's a lot one can learn from books. I look forward to your arbitration. Almost there." He grinned as the vehicle churned its way towards the airship.

Verity was surprised as they approached the main airship. What had seemed like a bulky, imposing craft at a distance was really small and agile, no more than an air cutter built more for speed than aggression. She could see where the gondola had been modified for warfare with extra weapons and reinforced plating, but it was quite a smart craft with neat lines. The envelope had clearly seen battle, and what had seemed like a smooth field of black from her bedroom window was, up close, held together with patches and repairs. A small round deck protruded from the gondola for the musca to land upon. Despite the tumultuous flight, Verity was shocked at how smoothly the driver landed the transport. She heard the hiss of its engines powering down and the resounding click of the safety mechanism being engaged to make sure it didn't fall off the ship. As soon as the musca had settled, Abraham popped out of his seat, leapt out of the carriage, and held the door wide for Verity. She gingerly lifted her skirt and, clinging to her flag, stepped out of the carriage onto the landing deck.

"M'lady," said Abraham with a slight bow, "may I introduce Captain Eli Calahan."

Despite Prudence's protestations to the contrary, Verity was well versed in the tales of airship pirates. She had read about Eli Calahan, his gentlemanly ways with prisoners, his code of honor and integrity. The authors that chronicled his adventures triumphed him as a man of nobility, often better than his adversaries from the upper classes. However, she knew what to expect from airship pirates—greasy, unkempt, filthy dregs of humanity. The airship pirates she had met so far had validated these expectations.

She was certainly not expecting to meet a fictional character in flesh and blood, and she most assuredly was not expecting him to be leg-weakeningly handsome. Today was a most interesting day.

"Captain," Verity said, curtseying.

The captain bowed elegantly, more elegantly than many of her father's friends had ever greeted her, and certainly more than she would expect from an airship pirate. Verity almost tripped over herself in shock and amorousness. He was stunning, a near-perfect specimen of manhood. He had long brown hair with auburn highlights, tied back neatly with a leather thong. Instead of the rugged and rough-hewn uniforms worn by the crew, the captain was adorned with a near fashionable elegance. He sported beige Cossack trousers with a tweed waistcoat and a chocolate brown tailcoat. His shirt collar was unbuttoned, but his clothes were impeccably maintained, and he stood out like a radiant jewel among the dust and rabble of his ship and crew.

"Lady Wheelwright," he said, extending his hand, "welcome aboard The Devil's Grog. Would you do me the honor of joining me for dinner?"

Verity gasped at the brazenness of the invitation. Her city was on fire, and she was a captive and potential slave for this man's lust, and possibly that of his crew, and he was inviting her to dinner? But for an instant, visions of fine dining and waltzing the evening away with this becoming figure of a captain flooded her imagination. Fortunately, Abraham interrupted and brought her back to reality.

"Begging your pardon, captain," he said, "but the lady wields the drapeau blanc and has demanded arbitration."

"Indeed?" said the captain with a smirk, cocking one eyebrow. "Well then, we must honor the laws of Grotius. M'lady, state your terms."

Verity hadn't thought this far ahead and began to stammer. In all honesty, she hadn't thought her ruse would work at all, and had expected the pirates invading her home were going to do God knew what with her. All she had planned was a distraction to keep her staff safe. But here she was, mere feet from an intoxicatingly handsome airship pirate of legend, being asked to deliver terms for her city. Fortunately, her years of tutelage had prepared her enough to improvise for situations such as this.

"I demand a cessation of hostilities against New Lutetia. You will cease your attack, withdraw your troops, and leave this airspace at once. What treasures you have already claimed will be yours to keep." She paused, gulping for air to steady her nerves. She knew full well that arbitration required an exchange and negotiation, and she steeled her nerves to offer her only bargaining chip. "You will harm no citizen, and will take no prisoner, save myself. My father is, as I'm sure you know, quite wealthy and influential, and would certainly pay a substantial ransom for my safe return."

The captain stroked his sharply chiseled jaw and turned to Abraham. "What do you think, Screw? We stop all this fuss and nonsense, take what we've got already, and bugger off for ports unknown with this lady in tow."

Abraham seemed to ponder the offer himself. "I don't know, captain. That's a lot to give up for just pocket change and herself. The boys'll expect their fair share of the loot as per their contract. Plus, I don't know if her father would pay up for her so willingly. Seems more likely than not that we'll have a whole fleet of gendarmes after us before he pays up."

"Agreed," said the captain, then turned back to Verity. "I'm afraid I'm unwilling to accept your terms, Lady Wheelwright. My men need to be paid for their services, and I can't divvy you up amongst the crew. Plus, there's no guarantee that your father will pay for your return. Take her back to her manor, Screw, and see that she is not harmed until she gets there." He turned and began to walk back slowly towards the main deck.

Abraham saluted, then shouted, "You heard the captain, Chillum. Get that musca ready to fly. We'll be escorting the lady back to her manor."

Chillum chucked as he started to poke at the controls of the transport. "What's she going to do once we get her there safely?"

"None of our concern, is it Chillum," Abraham said with a shrug. "Captain said get her there safely. Didn't say to guard her once she was down. Lady'll be on her own to fend for herself."

Verity panicked and shouted after the captain, "One million livres!"

The captain stopped and turned slowly on his heel.

"Excuse me?"

"My dowry," said Verity quickly. "When I turn twenty-five, which is less than two years away, my dowry becomes my personal property under law. It is invested and should exceed one million livres by then. I swear to you, by the laws of Hugo Grotius, on the grave of my dead mother, if you cease your attack on New Lutetia and promise never to return to its airspace again, if you promise to deliver me to my father's plantation in Bourbonia on the New Continent, I will not entertain a proposal of marriage for the next two years and deliver you my full and complete dowry upon my twenty-fifth birthday."

"Two years?" the captain sneered. "You expect me to wait two years for payment?"

"Please, sir," Verity said, "I have nothing else to offer. I know my father will pay for my return, and if he doesn't, my dowry is yours."

"One million livres can buy a lot of patience," muttered Abraham with a wink to the captain. "Plus, there's nothing to stop us working between now and then."

"Perhaps," said the captain. "Very well. Screw, call the men back. Divvy up what treasure we've claimed amongst the crew as is their due. We'll head for Bourbonia. Have the lady locked in my bedchamber. She will henceforth be claimed as my private prisoner and will be treated as such."

Abraham saluted smartly and began barking orders to everyone. Verity saw a flurry of activity before he unceremoniously grabbed her by the arm and began to drag her to the captain's bedroom.

"Unhand me, Mr. Screw," she said as she was marched across the deck, through the antechamber, and into the bedchamber. "I should be treated as a captive and prisoner of war. I'm not to be harmed."

"Well, there's the rub," said Abraham, tightening his grip

as he marched her forward. "Arbitration's over, so you're under the captain's law now. If he says lock you in his bedchamber, you'll be locked in his bedchamber. Plus, the laws of Grotius are all well and good, but you didn't mention being unharmed in your terms, so the captain can do whatever he wants with you. Plus, and this is most important," he continued as he forced her into the captain's bedchamber, "we're pirates. Don't sit much for laws and such, if you know what I mean."

"My Lady Wheelwright," bellowed the captain with a bold laugh right before Abraham slammed the bedchamber door in her face, "welcome aboard The Devil's Grog."

CHAPTER THREE: AN INVITATION

Verity looked around the bedchamber, which was expansive, considering the lithe size of the airship itself. There was an ample queen-sized bed, an oak wardrobe, a side table with two leather chairs, and a full dressing mirror. It was cozy, to be sure, and smaller than her own bedroom at home, but certainly more than Verity expected from an airship pirate.

Still in her green velvet gown, Verity sat in one of the leather armchairs. All of the excitement and adrenaline of the past hour, and surely it couldn't have been more than an hour, came crashing down about her. Her hands began to shake, and she put her head down on the table and began to sob. She was a prisoner, a captive of war, to a man who was, admittedly, ruggedly handsome but famed as much for his ruthless cruelty as his independent code of honor. She turned her head to look at the bed and began to shudder all over. While the livre rouge was quite explicit in their description of carnal acts, the women in those tomes had always been willing participants. Verity had no doubt in her mind what the captain had in mind. Still, she was a Wheelwright, and the representative of her city. She sat up, straightened her shoulders, and stared defiantly at the door. If she was to be ravished mercilessly by an airship pirate, so be it. She certainly wouldn't give them the satisfaction of her tears as well.

The longer she waited, the more angry and less frightened she became. The thought of being captured didn't bother her as much as the anxious waiting for her eventual torture. She drummed her fingers on the table and fidgeted with the lace on her sleeves.

A piece of paper slid under the door with a soft sibilance. Verity stood, slowly walked over, and picked it up. It was a simple piece of paper, folded and wax sealed. She looked at the mark in the crimson wax, half expecting a horned skull or similar. Instead, simple letters in a neat circle—ELC—were pressed into the wax. The mark was minimalist, stately almost. Verity pried the seal open with her thumb and read the letter, for it was a letter.

Lady Wheelwright,

I would like to formally welcome you aboard The Devil's Grog. Please allow me to apologize for our rough manners and brisk demeanors. We are working men and unaccustomed to entertaining elegant guests such as yourself.

I do hope that you will allow me to make amends by joining me for a private dinner this evening. Otherwise, I shall have the cook send you a tray when you are ready to dine.

I am aware that a lady such as yourself prefers to dress for dinner. You will find an assortment of gowns and dresses in the wardrobe. If I were to hazard a guess, I believe the canary silk will fit you well, and will also be most practical for an airship. I do not have a maid or servant to help you into your finery, but Screw will certainly lend a hand to necessary buttons. Rest assured your safety and virtue will not be threatened in any way.

Screw will knock on your door in approximately fifteen minutes. Please let him know your decision at that time.

Your Servant,
Captain Eli Callahan

Verity began to pace the room.
Dinner.
Dinner?
Here she was, sobbing her eyes out and waiting for a band

of pirates to hold her down and steal her virtue and that man, that contemptuous creature, dares to invite her to dinner. She exhaled heavily out her nose, stormed over to the wardrobe, and yanked the doors open.

A rainbow of dresses greeted her. Some were certainly too large for her, and many were years out of fashion, but they were in prime condition and quite respectable. She had expected moth-eaten rags or, worse, the scant shawls and uniforms of the ladies of Encornet. She pulled the canary yellow silk dress out to inspect it. It was a simple, high necked day gown with black lacing and beadwork. It was certainly not the formal style of dress she was accustomed to wearing to dinner, but it was less heavy than her green velvet, and, as the captain had pointed out, practical for an airship.

As she changed out of her green velvet and into the yellow silk, Verity reread the letter, which sat open on the table. Captain Callahan's script was a trained hand, and she wondered at the wording of the letter itself. The language and tone were much more elevated than she expected from an airship pirate, if the *livre rouge* were anything to be trusted. It wasn't a Boudician sonnet, to be sure, but it was polite and genteel, and piqued Verity's curiosity. What sort of man was Eli Callahan, really?

A sharp knock on the bedchamber door interrupted her ruminations.

"Is that you, Mr. Screw?"

"Yes, m'lady," said Abraham, sounding awkward and nervous, "Captain said I was to assist you with your gown, if necessary, and escort you to dinner. Assuming you want to join him, that is."

"Indeed," said Verity, pulling the dress up over her shoulders, "please feel free to enter. I will need help with these buttons."

She heard a key click and watched the door as the latch to

the bolt turned. The latch to the bolt. On her side of the door. *Oh, you silly nincompoop. You could've unlocked and opened the door at any time.* Why would the Captain's bedchamber have a lock on the outside of the door? What was she thinking?

And what exactly would you plan to do once you got the door open, she thought as the door swung in.

Abraham stood there, soldier erect, staring past her.

"M'lady," he said, "if you'd like to turn around, I'll do my best with your buttons."

Verity nodded and turned, exposing her back to Abraham, who hurried up to her and began working the buttons as quickly as possible. "I'm sorry, m'lady. I'll be as quick as I can," he said as he fumbled his way up her back and neck.

"You're doing fine, Mr. Screw. I thank you for your assistance." When he finished, Verity turned towards him.

He made quick eye contact, blanched, then stared past her face at the wall behind her.

"Well, Mr. Screw, shall we to dinner?"

"M'lady," he said, then offered his elbow to her.

Verity took it and together they stepped out of the Captain's bed chamber, through the antechamber, and onto the main deck.

A salt-perfumed breeze caught her face and teased her hair back from her cheeks. The Devil's Grog was a well-designed ship, and the balloon and the bow shields kept much of the wind away from the deck, but slight cross breezes still made their way through. Abraham, obviously more accustomed to airship life, held onto her arm with his other hand and escorted her gently forward.

"No worries, m'lady," he said, "it's a bit choppy on deck, but we won't lose you."

"I appreciate your kind attention, Mr. Screw," she said as they walked forward.

The few crew members on deck seemed to keep to their tasks, but Verity could feel their eyes following her through side glances. As they made their way forward to the dining cabin near the bow, Verity felt the pressure of their stares build up behind her.

"I have a feeling that I'm causing a small but silent uproar, Mr. Screw."

"Not to worry, m'lady," he said, "Captain gave us all a stern what for. They're just scared as to what'll happen if they step out of line. Plus, ain't too many of them have seen a lady such as yourself up close like this, so they're not sure whether to salute or shit themselves." He blushed. "Begging your pardon, m'lady."

"Mr. Screw," she said, patting his hand, "please do not worry about your language around me. I grew up around my father and his associates, and with enough brandy, they'd make even you blush."

They approached the door to the dining cabin, and Abraham opened it for her with a bow. Verity curtsied slightly at his dignified attempt and stepped inside.

The dining cabin was about the same size as the captain's bedchamber, but more oblong. It was a dark, oak paneled room adorned with delicate gas lamps. The table was small and set for two, but Verity could see the seam beneath the lace runner where it extended and made room for more dining guests. The chairs were high backed and functional, but not uncomfortable. Verity took this all in with a glance, then turned her gaze to the captain himself, who stood beside the table.

He had changed from his previous outfit and was adorned in perfect evening wear, his black tailcoat neat over his black waistcoat. A yellow cravat adorned his neck. Verity kept eyeing his square jaw and suspected he had even shaved for the occasion.

Captain Callahan bowed, then pulled out a chair, offering it to Verity. "M'lady, would you care to join me?"

Verity curtsied slightly and went to the chair. As she slipped past Captain Callahan, she could smell a hint of lime. He did shave for the evening. Interesting.

"Thank you, sir," she said, pulling the napkin onto her lap. Captain Callahan tugged on a rope next to the table and sat in his seat. He indicated a blown glass decanter in the center of the table.

"May I offer you some wine, Miss Wheelwright?" he said.

Verity cocked an eyebrow at the decanter and tilted her chin.

"It's not some exotic vintage from Oenotria, but it's passable. Better than the watered-down grog the crew's using to warm themselves up this evening."

Verity kept her gaze steady on Captain Callahan, almost daring him to make a wrong move.

"Well, fair enough. I can have the cook bring you up some sparkling water or something for dinner. I hope you won't mind if I indulge," he said, pouring himself a generous portion in a goblet. He took up the goblet, said "To your health, m'lady," and took a big gulp of the wine.

"I believe I shall partake of your wine, Captain," said Verity with an even voice.

"Oh, you will, will you?" He laughed, then poured her an equally hearty goblet of wine from the decanter with a flourish. "Seeing if I was going to poison you first, were you?"

"A lady in my situation can hardly afford to be too careful."

"I see," said Captain Callahan, meeting Verity's gaze. "Then let's settle this once and for all. You are my prisoner. We are agreed upon this, and it has been established by public arbitration in accordance with the laws of Grotius. I tell you this now. If you behave and do as you're told, on my life and honor, no harm will come to you until we deliver you safely to your father's plantation. The crew is under strictest orders to leave you alone. I will ensure that you are fed properly from what fare our stores can provide, and while it won't be the style of sustenance that you're accustomed to, it will certainly be quality food. You will have full rein of my bedchamber, but I'd ask you to confine yourself to those quarters, for your safety as well as that of the crew's. A woman aboard a ship is oft considered bad luck, but special exception is made for prisoners. That being said, the men might get distracted if they saw you meandering about the deck, so I'd ask you to stay confined to quarters. There is a lavatory in the antechamber, if you need that. I'll do my best to provide anything else you may need. These are my terms. Will you agree to them?"

Verity glared back at the Captain and said nothing.

"I see we're at an impasse," said the Captain, who took another gulp of wine. "So what will it take for you to be comfortable and enjoy this dinner with me?"

"How do I know you won't ravish me in my sleep?" said Verity. "How do I know you won't drop me off in some brothel in Encornet for a drink and a song to survive as best I can?"

Captain Callahan stared at her, clearly perplexed. Then he slowly spoke, "I can imagine, by your questions, that you've been reading one too many livre rouges. Let's get things straight. I'm not some lusty ne'er-do-well bent on conquering the loins of every woman I come across. My men, while possibly more ribald than the men you're acquainted with, certainly know better than to accost a prisoner. We are primarily businessmen. We have contracts, strike deals, make payments, and so forth. It's just that our income, primarily, comes from less than legal means, and so the gendarmes get a bit perturbed when we show up in their skies. But there will be no ravishing. Not on this voyage." He took a sip of wine. "Of course, if you want to be ravished like a lady in the livre rouge, I'm sure we could arrange something. We could get you out of that dress, tie you to a pole downstairs, and let the crew have its way with you. They are airshipmen, however, and more accustomed to rear entry, if legends are to be believed. That wouldn't bother you, would it?"

Verity gasped and put her hand over her mouth. She could feel the blush flood her cheeks. She had never heard anyone speak so boldly before—certainly none of the men her father did business with. These were the words straight out of a livre rouge, and she was shocked to hear them said aloud.

Captain Callahan laughed boldly and took another gulp of wine, almost draining his goblet. "A joke, m'lady, a joke. Forgive my impertinence. I was simply trying to lighten the mood. Please, do not worry. Confine yourself to my bedchamber and the antechamber, and no harm will come to you. Again, I swear it, on my life and honor."

"Captain Callahan," she said, "I would ask that you keep a civil tongue around me. I may be your prisoner, and you may be a pirate, but I think we should maintain a polite discourse." She couldn't help but smile slightly, and wished the gas weren't so bright as to expose her blush. She kept staring at Captain Callahan, his jaw, his neck, the black length of hair tied back with a black leather strap. She imagined tugging on that leather strap, then running her fingers through his thick locks. She imagined inhaling the lime aftershave that clung to his skin, breathing it in deeply and letting it intoxicate her. She took another sip of wine to cover her emotions and the fantasies that she was sure were clear on her face.

"I understand, m'lady." There was a sharp knock on the door. "Ah, dinner," he said, then shouted, "Enter!"

The door opened, and a large bald man covered with tattoos came into the room, carrying two covered trays. "Captain," he said, "as you ordered, from your private stores."

"Thank you," said Captain Callahan as the cook placed the trays on the table and pulled off the warming domes.

On each tray, a fine meal was prepared, much to Verity's

surprise. Each plate had two delicate quails, stuffed with what she thought was a cream and mushroom mixture, then roasted to perfection and glazed with an earthy and aromatic reduction. These had been served on top of a bed of wilted greens tossed with squash and apples and dressed with a piquant vinaigrette. Verity closed her eyes and inhaled the various aromas wafting off the plate.

"This smells most delicious, sir," she said to the cook.

He blushed. "Thank you, m'lady. Ain't much but humble air fare, but I hope you appreciate it." He turned to the Captain. "Will there be anything else, sir?"

"No," said Captain Callahan, "that will be all. I'll ring when we're finished." The cook nodded and left the room. "So," continued Captain Callahan, "where were we? I believe we were discussing your choice in literature and the lessons gleaned therein?"

Verity blushed again and took another sip of wine, trying to hide her face behind the wide curves of the goblet. She mustered her courage and tried to compose herself suitably before replying, "Captain, please forgive me. It's been a long and trying day. I do not wish to be rude, but I'd much prefer to dine in silence and enjoy this meal than to spoil it with coarse conversation. I believe the voyage to Bourbonia is quite lengthy, even in a vessel as sleek as this one, and there will be plenty of time for discourse between now and then."

"Well, I'm not one for quiet dinners, but if you wish to dine in silence, so be it. I certainly will not force you to converse with me. Please let me know when you've finished your meal, and I'll have you escorted back to my bedchamber."

And so they ate in silence. As much as Verity felt that conversations with her captor, a notable airship pirate, would be awkward and daunting, a meal in silence across the table from him was even more uncomfortable. Captain Callahan was ever true to his word and said nothing throughout the meal beyond politely offering to refill her wine glass. When she had refused that, he shrugged and set the decanter aside, not filling his goblet either.

Verity was sure that the meal was equally uncomfortable for him. She watched him eat, trying to discern information about him. She could tell that while he was trained in decent table manners, he was not accustomed to them, and that he was deliberately trying to pace his eating with her own. Certainly, were he alone, a small meal such as this would have been consumed quickly and ravenously in mere minutes, and he would be off performing other duties around the ship within moments of completion. She watched him toy with his quails, slowly carving them into manageable bites and dipping the tender meat in the creamy stuffing. She could tell that he was also trying his best not to stare at her and was focused on his food and plate more than any normal person would have been during a dinner, even though she was boldly staring at him and scrutinizing his every move.

When she had finished her meal, which tasted even better than it had smelled, she neatly folded her napkin beside her plate and said, "Thank you, Captain Callahan, for a delicious dinner. I believe I have finished."

A look of relief poured over Captain Callahan's face. "Have you now?" he said, rising from the table and coming around to help her from her chair. "Well then, what would a lady such as yourself prefer to do after dinner?" His deep baritone voice was throaty from such a rich meal and caused a slight tremble in Verity's thighs.

She did her best to maintain her composure. "Well, the gentlemen would probably retire to the billiard room for brandy and cigars, while the ladies would retire elsewhere for a game of cards, or maybe even herbal tea. Certainly, we would not see each other again until morning."

"I'm afraid we have a small ship, m'lady, and neither a

billiard room nor a card room. I'm sure we have some tea somewhere aboard, if that's your pleasure. I don't go in for cigars, myself. I'm more of a pipe man, on the occasion that I do partake, but I find qunubu tends to dull the senses a bit too much for my taste. So, will it be tea then, m'lady?"

"I think I shall have to decline," said Verity, "as it's been quite a long day."

"What say you to a dance, then, m'lady?"

"A dance? Good sir, you jest. I'm certainly not dressed for a ball, nor would I imagine there's enough room on this ship for a spirited galopade or Portland."

Captain Callahan pulled a cord on the wall and smiled. "No, m'lady, not a ball. Just a dance." There was a knock on the door, which Captain Callahan quickly opened. Abraham stepped in, carrying an accordion. He tipped his hat and bowed to both Verity and the Captain, then quickly pushed the dining table against the wall and sat next to it in one of the chairs. Captain Callahan turned back to Verity and smiled. "Would I be correct in assuming you know how to waltz?"

As Abraham began the opening chords of a slow folk waltz, Verity smiled and nodded. With no wine glass to hide her obvious blush, she simply took Captain Callahan's hand and put her other hand on his shoulder. This close to him, she could smell the lime aroma of his shaving balm and wanted nothing more than to taste the sweetness along his neck and jaw. She quivered with anticipation at his touch, at being pulled to his body, the press of his flesh against her flesh.

However, between that and the wine with dinner as well as the excitement of the evening, she could already feel herself slipping into an exhausted fog. She leaned onto Captain Callahan as he led her around the small room in a simple box waltz. She had been to balls before, of course, and was trained in all the modern dances. She knew a Viennese Waltz with all its elegant twists and spins across a ballroom. This was not that sort of dance. This was a simple folk dance, with the same basic step, but a softer, more intimate tone in the music and a closeness between partners that would be looked down upon in more genteel society. There were no dizzying fleckerls or underarm turns, but Verity was light-headed enough from the press of Captain Callahan's body to hers. As the music slowed to its final notes, Verity pulled back and looked deep into his sapphire eyes, which sparkled in the gaslight.

"There now," he whispered, "that wasn't so painful, was it?"

Verity shook her head. "No, Captain," she whispered back.

"Then let's get you to bed," he said, and turned to Abraham. "Screw, please escort Lady Wheelwright to her bedchamber." He turned and bowed deeply to Verity. "M'lady, I wish you a pleasant and restful good evening. If you need anything, please let Screw know, and we'll do our best to accommodate. Also, in the future, please refer to me as Eli." He then turned and marched out the dining cabin door.

"Eli," Verity whispered, tasting the name on her lips as she stared after him.

"M'lady," said Abraham, offering his elbow, "in your own time."

"Thank you, Mr. Screw," she said, and took his elbow, allowing him to escort her back across the breezy deck to the bedchamber. As they were walking, she asked, "Mr. Screw, can I inquire as to the name of the song you were playing?"

"Oh that?" he chuckled. "Just an old song from Clovisia. Based on a poem, I think. It's called *Plaisir d'amour.*"

"The pleasure of love lasts but a moment, while the grief of love lasts a whole lifetime," recited Verity.

"M'lady?"

"It's from a novel, Mr. Screw. A young man is mourning the loss of his love, Sylvia, to another man."

"I wouldn't know, m'lady. Not much of a reader. Just

know it's a favorite of the captain's." He walked her through the antechamber and into the bedchamber. "Well, goodnight, m'lady. If there's anything you need, just pull that red rope there next to the bed." He indicated a tasseled burgundy cord. "That'll sound my alarm, and I'll be with you quick as possible."

"Thank you, Mr. Screw," said Verity with a curtsey. He bowed and walked out the door, locking it behind him.

Verity opened the wardrobe and found a cotton nightgown that would fit her. She was half tempted to pull the cord to get Abraham here as she fumbled with the buttons on the back of her dress, but she was able to pry enough of them open to squeeze the silk over her head. She donned the nightgown and climbed into the expansive bed. "Plaisir d'amour," she hummed to herself as she slipped off to sleep.

CHAPTER FOUR: THE DUEL

Sunlight danced across Verity's face in warm beams filtered through the thick glass of the cabin window. She rolled over in the bed and stretched her arms over her head in a wide yawn. She had been on airships before, giant travel liners back and forth to the New Continent where bedrooms were pampering buffets of comfort and relaxation, but this had been one of the most luxurious sleeps she'd had in a long time. She felt sure the wine had something to do with it, as well as the dance.

The dance! Verity closed her eyes and dreamt of holding Captain Callahan — Eli — in her arms again. What she wouldn't give for another slow waltz with him, his muscled torso leading her strongly through the steps. Perhaps being a pirate's prisoner wasn't the most horrible fate. It was certainly more exciting than being tutored at her father's manor.

Verity rose from bed and began her morning rituals. She opened the wardrobe to find something suitable to wear for the day. She chose a simple day dress, which she slipped into quickly, and was about to go out into the antechamber when there was a vigorous pounding on the door.

"M'lady," Abraham all but shouted through the door, "we have a bit of a situation. You might hear some noise. Sit tight and stay locked in your room, and you'll be quite safe."

Verity's heart began to race. There was certainly a note of concern in Abraham's voice, and possibly doubt too. Verity called back, "Is everything quite alright, Mr. Screw?"

The voice that responded was not that of Abraham and

made it clear that things certainly were not alright. A deep, snarling voice with a pronounced Clovisian accent bellowed, "So we've found the captain's *salope* at last. Good, good . . ." There was a rattling of the doorknob as someone tried to enter the room. "He's got you sealed up good and tight, like a sweet *gateau* in a pretty cage. Why don't you come out of there, *mon petite gateau*, and we can all take a lick of your sugar." The speech was slurred and hollow, almost as though its speaker were sick.

"M'lady," shouted Abraham, "do not open the door!"

Verity heard various curses from the other side of the door. There were loud thumps, as if something were being thrown against the walls of the antechamber, followed by a crack of breaking wood. This was followed by a violent banging on the bedchamber door. Once again, Verity heard the accented voice. "So, *mon gateau*, your hero Screw is, shall we say, incapacitated the moment. You have a choice, then. You can unlock this door, come out willingly, and let the crew take what's owed from you, or I'll break down this door and take it myself, only twice as hard as necessary, and then I'll slit your pretty white throat just to watch you bleed out. So, what's it going to be?"

Verity's heart was in her throat. Up until this point, Abraham had been a gentleman. A bit rough around the edges, and maybe uncultured, but certainly polite and respectable. Furthermore, he seemed to answer only to the captain, and the rest of the crew seemed to jump at his beck and call. If he had come to her rescue, and not Eli himself, then God only knew what had happened on deck. She had Eli's word that she wouldn't be harmed, but if he was also incapacitated or worse, dead, then there was nothing stopping these men from pressing their advantage and then killing her for sport. The only choice she had was to leave the bedchamber of her own accord and hope that they would spare her life.

"I'm unlocking the door, sir," Verity said loudly and clearly. She reached for the lock on the door, clicked it open, and swung the door wide.

A mangy pirate swayed in front of her. In one hand he held a saber, and in the other hand a brown bottle of what, from the smell of it, was cheap spiced rum.

"Very good, very good," he said, "come on out, *mon petite gateau*. We just want what's ours."

Verity stepped forward and, more quickly than she had imagined possible, the pirate had sheathed his saber and was behind her with a hand on her shoulder. He began twirling his fingers through her hair and whispered, "*Mon petite gateau*, you smell delicious." Then, he reached down and squeezed her buttock with one firm, rough grip. "I could eat you up right here and now. Wouldn't you like that? Wouldn't you like to know what my tongue could do to you?"

Verity shuddered with fear and disgust but maintained her composure as best she could. "What would your crewmates say, sir, if you feasted without them?"

"Those *branleur* don't deserve a fine treat like you, do they now?" the man said with a snicker. The stench of spiced rum and tooth rot coming off his breath was pungent. "But we must all keep to the agreement, signed and sealed. Walk," he commanded as he clamped his hand tight on Verity's shoulder and shoved her forward toward the deck.

The whole crew had amassed on the deck, and her captor began bellowing to them as soon as they were in view. "Look what we have here, mates. Look what the captain's been keeping for himself, all private-like in his cabin." There was a round of chuckles and some whistles from the crew. "Now, when I signed on, I do remember signing a contract of servitude, a gentleman's agreement amongst brothers. One share of all Prizes for the crew, it says, writ there in ink and signed in blood. But it looks like our captain's been keeping the prizes to himself, don't it? So, I'm here to claim my prize, right here and now, and any man who says otherwise will taste my steel!"

There was a crash at the other end of the deck, and the door to the dining cabin burst off its hinges. Eli stepped forth. "The Captain," he said, "shall have one full share and a half of all Prizes, Bug Face. That there's more than one and half shares of what we claimed in New Lutetia. I claim it as my own, but if you insist on blades, let it be so." He drew his own sword with a swift and deft motion that Verity had rarely seen, even from her father's most regarded fighters.

The pirate who held her shoulder shoved her away. She turned and saw him take a giant swig from his bottle, then smash it to the deck and draw his own sword. "I've been looking to this for a long time," he chuckled. "You've gone soft, you *lavette*. We need a new captain around here, not one that's going to take orders or arbitrate with a trumped-up *poufiasse* with a flag. I'm going to gut you, then gut that *debile* in there that thinks he's above us all just because he's first mate, and then I'm going to take this ship and raid every city up and down the New Continent until I'm rich as a king with twice his harem."

"Fine plan," said Eli, waving his sword, "but can you follow through?"

With that, the pirate leapt at Eli and the duel engaged. Verity gasped as the swords clashed against each other. She had seen fencing duels performed for her father, of course. But they were nothing like this. This was less genteel and less elegant, lacking all the finesse and gallantry of fencing. Eli and the other pirate were using formations that she was familiar with, but grunting and swearing at each other, too. Their moves were jerky and unrefined, and their duel turned in circles and roamed all over the deck. She realized, suddenly, what the men who fenced before her father were practicing for. They were not training to survive but training to kill each other. Eli was aiming to kill this other man, right here, in cold blood. And he was struggling mightily to do it.

The other pirate clearly had the upper hand in the duel. While Eli was certainly holding his own, he was barely able to parry the other man's assaults, and certainly was unable to riposte from that and gain any sort of advantage. The other pirate knew he was winning and pressed harder, often swinging wildly in an attempt to slash Eli open instead of simply stabbing him. Even though he was clearly intoxicated, often stumbling and swerving in his attacks, he was still quicker and more agile than Eli. And he knew it.

"So, the Cavalier Eli Calahan is losing his touch, is he?" the pirate said as he slashed wildly at Eli again. "Maybe he's spent too much time dancing and romancing our treasure to be bothered with keeping up his training, eh boys?" There was no response from the crew, but Verity could sense some anxiety. She wasn't sure how much of this mutiny was supported out of loyalty to the other pirate as much as it was fear of what he would do if they didn't back him.

There was another slash, and Eli stumbled and tripped over his own feet. He fell down on the deck, the sword clattering out of his hand. The other pirate sneered and stepped over him, blade poised to kill. "Thus ends the legacy of Cavalier Eli Calahan."

There were three sharp pops from behind Verity, which she realized were shots from a revolver. She gasped as the other pirate dropped his sword, stumbled backwards, and fell dead. Then she screamed and ran towards Eli.

"What exactly did you plan to do, m'lady?" he whispered, then sat up, struggling to his feet. They both turned and saw Abraham leaning on the doorpost to the antechamber, one hand holding his head, the other a pepperbox pistol. "Much obliged, Screw."

"Lads," Screw said, stumbling out of the doorway, still holding his head, "the agreement that we signed, our code of brotherhood, states that if at any time you meet with a prudent Woman, any Man that offers to meddle with her without her Consent, shall suffer present Death. Lady Wheelwright is a guest of our Captain and, on my honor, a prudent woman. She denied Bug Face's advances, and I witnessed it. Does any man among you say otherwise?" A general murmur went through the crew. "I said, does any man among you say that Bug Face did not meet a just death in accordance with our agreement?" This time, the crew shouted their affirmation in one bellowing unison.

"Mr. Screw," said Eli, still panting heavily from his duel, "remind me again how much we claimed from New Lutetia."

"Quite a pretty penny, sir," said Abraham, "certainly enough to sustain the crew."

"And yet," continued Eli, "we have no place in which to sustain them, do we?"

"Well, we have provisions, sir, and grog."

"Yes, yes . . . provisions and grog will keep a man alive, but is that sustenance, Screw?" He turned towards the crew, still gathered on the deck. "I ask you, gentlemen, is mere food and drink enough to keep a man going beyond mere existence? Did we join this life of piracy simply to survive, or are we meant to thrive? I did not become a pirate simply to eke out a living, but to drink fully from the cup of life, to sample her every bounty and enjoy her every pleasure." There were nods and murmurs of assent throughout the crew, and Eli continued. "Mr. Screw, I believe our men are wont for all the pleasures of life, and they have been withheld these pleasures for far too long. We are due, therefore, for a quick detour. Adjust your heading and make haste! We aim for Encornet!"

A cheer erupted from the crew, loud enough to cover Verity's gasp of shock. Encornet? That was the most debauched nest of lust and gluttony in the entire world, if her books were to be believed.

"Three cheers for the captain," barked Abraham, leading the crew in a hip-hip-hooray. "And one more for Encornet," he said, to a laugh and another hooray from the crew. "Now get to work, you dogs, and somebody get this filth off our deck." He nodded to the corpse. Two crewmen quickly ran up, grabbed the body under the armpits, and unceremoniously threw it over the side of the ship. The whole crew crossed themselves, blew a kiss to the sky, and continued with their work.

Verity stared horrified at Eli, who smirked. "Burial at sky, m'lady. Bug Face was cruel, even evil, but he was still an airshipman. We send him off into the element which sustained him, and may God have mercy on his soul. Now, I believe you were unceremoniously roused from your slumber, and have not had time to compose yourself this morning. If you'd like to rest more, feel free; otherwise, take your time and prepare yourself, and then, if you're willing, join me for breakfast."

Eli turned and began to walk away, but Verity said, "Captain, sir. About Encornet . . ."

Eli turned back to her and grinned. "Lady Wheelwright, I'm sure you have heard rumors about Encornet and perhaps have even read about that city. Let me assure you, whatever you've heard barely scratches the surface. Encornet is a sprawling metropolis of extravagant food and rampant gambling. The very air is steeped with the aroma of blood and lust. With enough coin, a man can sate every depraved and reprobate whim that would shock even the demons of Hell, and believe me, we have coin enough to spare." He paused to give Verity a polite bow. "And you, m'lady, shall be my guest of honor. Onward, to Encornet!"

CHAPTER FIVE: ENCORNET

The docking tower in Encornet was not what Verity expected. It was clean, for starters. Impeccably so. She had seen more poorly maintained towers on vacation spots and military bases when she accompanied her father, and certainly more poorly constructed. This was a sturdy tower of steel, with various safety precautions and guardrails in place. The dock attendant stood at attention and saluted Eli as he stepped off the airship, arm locked tight around Verity.

"Captain Callahan, welcome back to the Free Municipality of Encornet. Will this be a routine visit?"

"Just an overnight to relax and reload, my good man," said Eli, tossing him a bag of coins. "That there says no one will come near my boat except them that works it, and your honorable self, of course. The standard supplies will do. No need for frills and lace. We'll be getting enough of that on shore, if you know what I mean. The list's in the bag. As always, you may retain the surplus for yourself."

"Most generous, Captain," said the dock attendant, weighing the bag with an expert hand then pocketing it. He bowed as Eli and Verity walked past to the stairs. Or what Verity thought would be stairs. Instead, they entered a small room, where an attendant bowed and closed the door neatly behind them, trapping the three of them in a tight, metal box. The attendant then pulled a lever, and the whole room shook and began moving. Verity shrieked, and both Eli and the attendant looked at her.

"First time in an elevator, m'lady?" asked Eli, clearly

surprised. Verity nodded, too scared to speak. "Don't worry. It's safe. Just think about it like a dumbwaiter, but instead of food and dishes, it carries people."

"Been working the shaft going on eight years now, m'lady" said the attendant with a pronounced Boudician accent. "My brother worked it five years before that. Ain't never had an accident."

"See?" said Eli, taking Verity's hand and giving it a soft squeeze. "Nothing to worry about."

Verity blushed at Eli's hand and looked out over the city. She had imagined Encornet would be a destitute wasteland of ramshackle buildings and winding alleys like the Cocotte district back in New Lutetia. Instead, it looked like a well-planned, organized town. Certainly not a teeming metropolis by any means, but not the lion's den of iniquity she had expected.

The elevator rattled to a stop at the base of the tower, and Eli tipped his cap to the attendant and flipped him a coin, which the attendant neatly caught and pocketed. "Obliged as always, Captain," he said, "I'll be here when you get back."

"Thank you, lad," said Eli as he wrapped his arm around Verity and walked her out the door. "If the crew gives you any trouble, you let me know, and I'll sort it out for you."

Eli manhandled Verity down the street, forcing her into a brisk march that almost stumbled her. "Captain," she said, almost out of breath, "is there a need to be so vigorous?"

"M'lady, this is Encornet. One must keep up appearances. You are my prisoner, and things will be expected. Behaviors must be maintained, attitudes displayed, and so forth, lest we rouse suspicion. I apologize in advance for anything that might happen, but I assure you the alternate would be worse."

This did not assure Verity. She had already seen a man killed on her behalf, so she couldn't imagine what would be expected in Encornet. She stared as she was marched past various establishments, all of which seemed to offer one sort of vice or another. She had expected taverns and gambling halls, to be sure, but she saw Sadozai opium parlors, and fighting dens where people could waste their money away as well. Restaurants offering exotic food from Bharat and Huaxia perfumed the air, and she even saw luxury shops offering specialties like jewelry and other trinkets.

Eli saw her stare and laughed. "M'lady, I'm sure that you have read a livre rouge, so I cannot imagine you are completely innocent. However, the authors of those tales tend to exaggerate for the sake of titillation, so allow me to correct some notions. Encornet is private municipality unbeholden to any Empire. It sets up its own taxes, and like its namesake, has arms in every business imaginable. It takes in all people of every race, creed, religion, as long as they're willing to pay. It is a safe haven, to be sure, for activities such as mine, as well as many other vices that other cities would question or exile to their slums.

"But to keep those vices safe and secure costs money, so Encornet taxes heavily and expects businesses to maintain a good reputation. Gold of any coinage is the ruler here, not allegiance to any crown or creed. A person can obtain any sin and pleasure in this municipality for a price, whether it be food, drink, gambling, gaming or fighting. But people have other wants and desires as well, and one can buy jewelry, art, books, silks and any other luxury you can imagine. If the world produces it and someone can sell it, it can be found in Encornet. Of course, there are other desires that men have, and those are what we pursue now. We journey to Nouvelle Pigalle."

Verity gasped. Nouvelle Pigalle was famous in livre rouge as the home of some of the most notorious and raunchiest brothels in the world. She had thought she was under the

Captain's protection, not his own private sex slave to enjoy in the privacy of house of ill repute. Her heart ached with betrayal as she was marched like a prize through the streets. They turned a series of corners and found themselves walking down a road of giant houses and storefronts.

There could be no question that they were in Nouvelle Pigalle. Never had Verity seen so much flesh displayed in so many debase ways. She wasn't completely innocent, surely, and understood that men and women had physical desires that needed to be sated, but to see those desires promoted and advertised like any other product was both shocking and, if Verity were completely honest with herself, exciting.

There were women, of course, bent over balconies and leaning in doorways, stroking their thighs and massaging their breasts to entice customers. There were men, too, glistening with oil spread over bulging muscles. Some were wearing only trousers, and some were wearing less than that, leaving very little to the imagination as to the size of their manhood and all the things that could be done with it. Then there were window displays of people dancing provocatively to entice customers, and even people tied with ropes or leather straps to beds and other devices, advertising more deviant pleasures to customers. As much as Verity was shocked at such brazen displays of lust for sale, she was also curious, and she couldn't stop staring. She imagined what it would be like to feel restrained like that, ropes tugging into her wrists as a lover took advantage of her helpless body. It was an idea that she hadn't even read about in a livre rouge, and the thought was exciting.

They marched down the street, Eli ignoring all the catcalls and whistles trying to get his attention and patronage until they came to a white building that occupied a corner lot. As opposed to the other establishments that Verity had seen on this street, this was a very humble and subdued building.

There were no men or women displaying their nakedness to entice customers, merely a set a of stairs leading up to a porch with ornate pillars. Everything had been designed to look as though it were made of marble, though Verity could clearly see where the paint was peeling from the wood.

"M'lady, welcome to the Temple of Aphrodite, the greatest establishment of rest and relaxation in the great municipality of Encornet. Tonight, you shall be my guest and will enjoy all the pleasures that the Corinthians have to offer." With that, Eli practically dragged Verity up the steps and through the doors of the brothel.

The interior of the room was as elegant and stately as the exterior was humble. Verity had expected women and men in various states of undress lounging around on couches for customers to choose from. She had expected the building to reek of musk and alcohol, a rich mix of lust aromas saturating the air. She had expected the walls to echo with the throaty sounds of passion as people coupled together in the various rooms of the establishment.

Instead, it was a simple long room, almost like a wide hallway, flanked with pillars. Two men stood at attention at the doorway, clearly there to keep out undesirables if necessary. In the center of the room, a woman in a white dress stood at a podium. Behind her a fountain bubbled delicately. Another woman sat on a stone bench beside it, fingering a soft melody on a harp. Beyond a few decorative plants in vases tastefully arranged around the room, there was little else.

"Captain Callahan," the lady said with a familial smile, "welcome back to the Temple of Aphrodite. Will you be partaking of your usual services this evening?"

"No," bellowed Eli in a jovial manner that Verity had never seen, "tonight is special, Ms. Ieriea. Tonight, I want nothing but the best. Take me to the peak of Olympus and show me pleasures known only to the gods!"

The lady's smile broadened with delight. "The Olympian service, Captain? How delightful. We aim to serve. Will you be needing company this evening?"

"Not tonight," said Eli, shaking Verity as if to show her off. "I brought my own, if you know what I mean."

"Most excellent." Ms. Ieriea clapped her hands, and from behind a pillar another woman appeared, also wearing a white dress. "Penelope will escort you to your room, Captain. Enjoy your stay."

The women both bowed, and Penelope turned and walked down the hallway. Eli grabbed Verity and half-walked, half-dragged her with him as they followed. They turned a corner and began to ascend a set of metal stairs tucked behind one of the pillars. Verity realized that the whole entry room was just for show, and that the pillars were designed to hide doorways and staircases. The impression was one of austerity and elegance rather than debased lust.

Penelope opened a thick oak doorway and ushered them into a mammoth room.

Verity was used to opulence as the daughter of a Lord and the head of New Lutetia. But she had never experienced splendor such as this. The room was actually four separate rooms. The first room, which they'd entered, was carpeted with a thick rug. Verity was wearing her boots but could only imagine what it would be like to step on such a plush cloth with her bare feet. There was a dining area with a round walnut table that could easily fit four people comfortably, even eight if they sat close and tucked in their elbows.

Penelope bowed, and opened a door to the right of the table, exposing a full bathroom with a marble-inlaid tub complete with indoor running water service, a full-length mirror, a sink, and even a flush toilet. The whole room smelled of talc and lavender. Penelope then opened the far door and ushered them into a magnificent bedroom. It was easily twice if not three times the size of Verity's bedchamber at the mansion in New Lutetia. The room was carpeted similarly to the entry room. On one side was a giant four-poster oak bed with a thick mattress, opulent pillows, and fresh sheets. On the other side of the room were two parallel meridiennes upholstered in rich velvet. A replication of the Venus de Milo stood in the corner, observing the room with her patient eyes.

Penelope bowed and said, "Please enjoy your stay, Captain."

She began to leave, but Verity said, "Wait! What's in the other room?" She indicated the door opposite the bathroom, which Penelope had neglected to open.

Eli chuckled, and Penelope blushed, then said, "The pleasure room, ma'am, is for the private use of our most honored guests. If either of you require assistance or would like to partake of our various services, please use the private speaking tube, and someone will attend to your pleasure immediately." Here she indicated a brass tube with a black mouthpiece that was hanging discretely beside the bed.

"Most excellent, Penelope," said Eli. "Please inform the staff that, unless we ask for assistance, we are to be undisturbed. Absolutely undisturbed."

"We value your privacy, Captain. If we can please or comfort you in anyway, let us know. Otherwise, you shall not know that we are here." With that, she bowed again, and stepped quietly out the room, locking the door behind her.

"Well," said Eli, walking over to unhook the speaking tube, "it's been a long day. Shall I order us an early supper, or would you prefer to rest first?"

Verity turned slowly, straightened her shoulders, and looked Eli squarely in the face. "Captain Callahan," she said, "I am your prisoner. I realize that you are a man with wants and needs, and if it is my lot to be forced to sate those needs, I will acquiesce without a struggle. But I refuse to enjoy it, and

I will do so only for the protection of the people of New Lutetia." She raised her chin slightly in the spirit of defiance and triumph.

Eli hung up the speaking tube, walked over to Verity, and took her gently by the shoulders. "Lady Wheelwright, I will attempt to explain this to you one last time. I am Captain Callahan. Cavalier Eli Calahan. On my honor, I will not touch you nor approach you in anyway unbecoming to a lady of your station. You are my prisoner, indeed, but more importantly you are my guest and a lady of honor and distinction. While I may have needs and desires, as does any man, they will not be taken out on you. This house, this entire street, is teeming with women that, for a few coins, could exhaust those desires sufficiently. I have no need to force you to do so. We are here, in this room, to escape the mean life of an airship, to enjoy one night of relaxation and luxury, and to hide away in safety from those that would pursue us. That is all. Now, I am hungry from our journey. I would like a decent meal. Would you care to join me?"

His face was mere inches from hers, the hints of lime balm and male musk tempting her nose. Were she any bolder, she would cross those inches with her lips and kiss him, full and hard, just to have one moment of wanton adventure before she died. She would dig her fingers into his back, pulling his muscled torso against her, letting her passions take the reins of her desperate flesh for one glorious moment. But she was not a harlot out of the pages of a livre rouge but a lady, so she nodded, curtsied, and said, "I would enjoy a meal and your company, Captain Callahan."

Eli walked to the bed and unhooked the speaking tube again. He ordered two dinners to be sent up directly and received a muffled reply. Within minutes, there was a knock on the door to the room. "Let's dine," said Eli, and escorted Verity out of the bedroom to the table in the entry and dining area. He pulled a chair out for her and offered a hand to help her sit. Then he walked over and opened the door.

A young woman in a white dress entered, followed by a man in a white tunic. They both bowed, and the woman said, "My name is Callista, and this is Alexander. We will be serving your dinner this evening." They quickly and expertly dimmed the gas lamps in the room, lit tapers in crystal holders on the table, then set the table, laying out silverware and napkins, setting up stemware and pouring two glasses of sparkling mineral water. Verity was used to being served, of course, but usually by a staff that was dressed in formal evening wear and doing their best to remain out of sight and unobtrusive. Callista and Alexander, however, were making a performance of it, almost dancing a ballet around the table as they set it for dinner. Once it was prepared, Alexander slipped out of the room, and returned with two small plates.

"Your first course this evening will be a Bartlett pear poached in spiced brandy with a swirl of vanilla-enriched mascarpone and sprinkled with candied lemon zest. We have paired this with a dry cabernet." Alexander poured the wine, then retreated to the hallway while Callista stepped back in the corner, allowing for more intimacy and privacy.

The pears were small, but juicy from the poaching liquid. Between the alcohol in the fruit and the warmth of the wine, Verity was immediately drawn into the meal, and ate politely but voraciously. She watched in silence as Eli ate and slowly sipped his wine. The pears were sweet and tart, leaving her lips wet and ready to kiss.

Once they had finished, Callista clapped her hands, and Alexander returned, deftly clearing their plates and replacing them with two larger plates.

"Your entrees," said Callista, "are simple steaks seasoned with the chef's own blend, drizzled with a blue cheese reduction, and topped with wild mushrooms and cipollini onions.

He has accompanied the meat with asparagus flavored with a walnut crema and sprinkled with pecorino tartufo. It will be served with a rich, full-bodied zinfandel."

Verity was used to coursed dinners, certainly, but never like this. These portions, a steak that covered almost two thirds of the plate and a generous helping of earthy asparagus spears with a pungent cheese, were almost too much. She would normally have had a quarter of this food per course, and rarely would it have been served in such a simple way. The whole room swelled with the musky aromas of the vegetables, which Verity was familiar with, but had never seen prepared so boldly.

A mushroom at her mansion would have been stuffed and breaded or delicately sautéed on their own and served by themselves. She would normally have two or three on a plate, and they would serve as the prelude to another course, then another. Never would they have been slathered on a steak like this with tiny round onions in a pungent blue cheese sauce. When she bit into one, all the meaty flavors, enhanced by the blue cheese, filled her mouth. She sliced her steak, and the juice spread across the plate. The meat was still pink, almost red, and she looked at Eli in shock.

"It's fine," he said, "it's just rare. Trust me, it won't hurt you at all. Try it. It's quite good."

Verity cut off a small piece towards the edge that was slightly less red than the rest of the meat and put it in her mouth. Her eyes almost rolled back into her head with pleasure. There was a flavor to the meat, something sweet and spicy and fiery all at once, that bombarded her tongue and enhanced every sensation in her mouth. The steak itself was not dry or leathery as she was used to, but juicy and tender, and practically melted in her mouth like butter. She heard Eli chuckle as she took another, more generous bite, then another and another.

Once that course had been completed, Alexander whisked back into the room at Callista's beckoning, swept the empty plates and glasses away, and returned with two goblets of a dark, rich mixture.

"For your dessert, the chef has prepared a chocolate mousse perfumed with vanilla and bourbon. This will be served with a tumbler of Hibernian liquor."

Eli began to eat, but Verity eyed the plate warily. She was used to jellies and puddings and tarts, nothing like this. "What is this?" she whispered.

"It's chocolate mousse," said Eli, "it's like a creamy custard, but with chocolate. Go ahead. It won't bite you."

Verity took a small spoonful of the brown stuff between her lips and let it settle on her tongue. She moaned, audibly moaned, at the velvety texture and dark, bitter flavors brought under control by the sweet vanilla and alcohol tastes. There was something sensual about this dessert, a sweet lusciousness that hinted at a dark, brooding side bubbling underneath. She almost abandoned all table manners as she quickly ate the rest of the dessert while Eli watched, grinning at her voraciousness. "That," she said, "was incredible." She grabbed the short glass of wine and took a big gulp to clear her throat.

"No, wait!" said Eli, but it was too late. The amber liquid in the goblet baptized Verity's mouth and throat with a sweet fire that tore down to her belly. She almost dropped the glass on the table as she began to cough and choke. Eli jumped up and ran around the table to hold her shoulder and tap her on the back as she continued to sputter and gasp for breath, laughing all the while.

"Is that brandy?" she said between wheezing fits.

"Sort of," said Eli. "Brandy is like wine, only stronger. This is from Hibernia and is made with barley, mostly. It's for sipping, not for drinking. Take your time. Have some water." He looked up at Callista. "She's fine. You go on ahead. Leave the goblets for later."

Callista nodded, and left the room, locking the door behind her while Eli continued to pat and rub Verity's back between her shoulders. She sipped the water, letting its mineral flavors clean the taste of the whiskey. "Do people really enjoy that?" she said, still trying to get her breath under control.

"Of course, just not all at once," said Eli, sitting down and sipping his own glass. "They people of Hibernia call it *uisce beatha*, or water of life. It's meant to be sipped and enjoyed. Try it again, only slowly. Small sip, just enough to coat your tongue."

"Well, it certainly is invigorating," said Verity, taking up the glass. "Again." With that, she took a small sip and let the amber liquid coat her tongue. It still burned, but this time Verity got lost in the complexity of the flavors. It was sweet, to be sure, with fruity flavors reminiscent of wine, but there was an edge to it that tasted, pleasantly, of smoke and fire. As it filled her mouth, Verity tasted dessert flavors, like vanilla and honey, and understood the pleasure of such a beverage after a meal. She certainly would no longer be satisfied with tea after dinner, that was to be sure. "I believe," she said, taking another, larger sip, "that I could come to enjoy this very much. I thank you for opening up my horizons, Captain Callahan."

"M'lady," he said, raising his glass to her then swallowing the rest of its contents in a quick gulp. "Now, we have dined. I would suggest that we take full advantage of this establishment for the evening and introduce you to all the pleasures that Encornet has to offer." He stood up and marched to the door which had, up until then, remained closed, and swung it open.

Verity's heart leapt. "Captain," she said, "you promised . . ."

Eli cut her off. "M'lady, I gave my word. I will not break

that. I need you to trust me." He stepped over to her and took her hand. "You can do that, can't you? You can trust me?"

Verity nodded and allowed Eli to take her gently by the hand and lead her into the room.

She didn't know what to expect, but it certainly wasn't this. The gas lamps that lit the room were hidden behind panes of red glass, so that a crimson glow adorned everything. In the center of the room was chaise longue upholstered in dark leather, but it was wider than normal, and was on a platform that elevated it to waist height. There were a few other pieces of furniture in the room, and a dressing screen in the corner, but beyond that, it was pretty sparse.

"M'lady, wait here." Eli went back into the bedroom and said something, presumably into the speaking tube next to the bed. Verity wandered around the room, looking at its contents from every angle, trying to discern what they could possibly be for, when she heard a knock at the door. Eli opened it, and said, "Come in!" Verity watched as he escorted a young woman into the room, dressed in the same white dress as the other employees. "This is Lydia, and she is skilled at the art of pleasure. I am going to see enjoy another glass of that delicious Hibernian liquor, so I leave you in her capable hands. Do what she says, m'lady, and trust me." With that, he stepped out of the room.

"M'lady," said Lydia, indicating the screen, "if you would prefer to undress, there is a gown behind there."

Undress? Verity balked visibly at the suggestion, but Lydia continued. "Please, m'lady, I promise you will enjoy this. The Captain has asked me to attend to you, and I will do so."

Verity nodded and stepped behind the screen and unbuttoned her dress. Folded neatly on a small table was a white silk robe. It was austere, but elegant, and Verity enjoyed the feeling of the silk against her skin. She stepped out from behind the screen, where Lydia was waiting.

"If m'lady would care to lie down," she said, indicating the chaise longue. Verity began to sit, and Lydia shook her head. "No, m'lady, the other way. Lie down on your belly." Verity followed the instructions, the silk robe beginning to fall off of her and expose her naked flesh. Lydia expertly pulled the robe away with one hand, immediately replacing it with a warm towel in the other hand, so that Verity was still modestly covered.

Lydia pulled a small metal bowl from one of the drawers, then struck a match and lit something in it. She reached back into the drawer and tossed a scoop of powder into the bowl, which immediately began to smoke, filling the room with a pungent aroma. She quickly capped the bowl and hung it from a chain, the smoke still streaming out from tiny holes in the lid. "Incense, m'lady, from exotic lands. Close your eyes and allow it to awaken your senses."

Verity closed her eyes and let the spicy woody aromas fill her nostrils and lull her into a relaxed state. She hardly noticed when Lydia pulled back the towel from her shoulders and said, "We'll begin."

Lydia placed her hands on Verity's shoulders and began to slowly stroke her skin. It was a gentle touch at first but became increasingly more vigorous. There was some sort of oil on her hands that made her touch smooth and slick, and she began kneading Verity's back with deep, practiced motions.

Verity sighed and moaned in delight as all the pressure and ache in her body began to melt away under Lydia's skilled ministrations. Her fingertips travelled up and down Verity's back and arms, the oil soaking into her skin until she felt completely cozy and untroubled by anything in the world. "Would m'lady like to stop here, or shall we continue?"

"Please continue," Verity practically begged. She had never felt so serene, almost as though her body had liquified into a luxurious pool of pleasure. Lydia pulled the tower further down, and Verity gasped as Lydia began to squeeze her backside. She immediately let out a throaty moan of salacious bliss as Lydia's fingers seemed to squeeze every drop of anxiety and tension out of her body, leaving nothing but delectation in its wake. Lydia moved down to her legs, and Verity could feel herself completely falling under the spell of this woman's touch. He whole body was limp and powerless with delight. Between the heady incense and the silky feel of the oil, Verity felt like a goddess who was being worshipped in a temple.

Lydia finished and pulled the towel back over Verity. "Take your time, m'lady. I'll leave the robe for when you're ready." She left quietly, and Verity slipped into a half-conscious doze of complete contentment.

The was a gentle knock on the door. Eli's voice came through. "Lady Wheelwright, I'm in no hurry, but I thought you should know that it's late in the evening and you would probably be more comfortable in the bed. Please take your time, though."

Verity sighed and slowly rose from her perch. She groggily slipped on the silk robe and tied it loosely about her. Her whole body still felt weak and languorous, and she half-drifted out of the room. Eli stood there, still dressed, as handsome and rugged as ever.

Verity said, "I believe I shall go to bed, Captain Callahan. Have a pleasant evening."

"I will join you shortly, Lady Wheelwright."

His words didn't register with her until her head sank into the pillow. The excitement of the past few days as well as the luxury and relaxation of this paradise had exhausted her thoroughly. Between that and the alcohol at dinner, which she was still feeling the effects of, she was completely useless and couldn't put up a resistance even if she had wanted to.

To make matters worse, she wasn't sure she wanted to

resist anymore. Here was the man she had been waiting for, a man she had only read about previously, a man whom she thought was only myth. He was literally in the next room. She had dined with him and danced with him. Verity realized, in that moment, that not only was she not afraid or repulsed by Eli, but she actually wanted him. She wanted to touch him and taste him. She wanted to learn about the world from him. Even if she only had between now and the New Continent, she wanted to partake of every pleasure he had to offer.

Verity undid the sash of her robe and pulled it open. She was ready to learn all there was about the pleasures of Encornet and wanted Eli as her private tutor.

She waited for him to join her in bed, and was still waiting when she finally succumbed to sleep.

CHAPTER SIX: SURRENDER

Verity was still groggy when a hand gently took her by the shoulder and shook her awake.

"Lady Wheelwright," said Eli, "it's time to go."

Verity stretched and looked out the window. It was still dark outside, and the morning sun hadn't even begun to pierce the horizon. "What time is it?" she said, yawning wide.

"It's quite early. I let you sleep for a few hours, and you can rest more on The Devil's Grog, but we must hurry. Please. I'll give you some privacy and allow you to get dressed."

Eli left the room and Verity rolled out of bed. In a haze of half-consciousness, she fumbled into her dress and shoes, and stepped into the main room of the suite. Eli was fully dressed and waiting for her.

"Did you enjoy your evening, m'lady?" he asked, taking her by the hand and walking her outside the room.

"I did. I thought you were going to join me in bed, though," she said, then gasped. What had she turned into, telling a man she wanted him in her bed? Was she some soiled dove of Encornet now, lulled into lust by gluttony and pampering?

"M'lady," said Eli, escorting her quickly down the stairs, "I'm sure I would very much have enjoyed that; however, you were deeply under the effects of the alcohol and there are rules about such things. Please hurry now. I've got a velocab waiting."

Eli tipped his hat to the two guards as they left the building, and Verity was ushered down the stairs and into the back of a velocab. She had seen such contrivances before but had never ridden in one. The back was like a rickshaw, and the front was the start of a bicycle, so that she and Eli could sit comfortably, enjoying the cool pre-dawn air as the driver peddled them towards the docking towers. Verity curled into Eli's chest, still barely awake, as the velocab wound its way through the municipality and ended at their tower. Eli paid the driver, then helped Verity down. He practically carried her into the elevator, then nodded at the attendant, who took them to the top of the tower. Despite the early hour, the dock attendant was present and apparently waiting for them.

"Are we all ready, my good man?" bellowed Eli as he walked towards the ship.

"Indeed, you are sir. I have procured everything on your list as requested."

"Thank you again for your expediency," said Eli, flipping the man a gold coin. "Your service was impeccable."

"Most generous," said the attendant, bowing as Eli helped Verity up the boarding ramp onto The Devil's Grog.

Abraham was waiting for them at the top of the ramp and took Verity by the arm. "M'lady, you'll be needing more sleep. Let me escort you to your room."

Verity nodded sleepily and allowed Abraham to escort her to the Captain's bedchamber, where she collapsed into a heavy slumber.

Verity awoke to a loud booming sound that rattled the windows of her bedchamber. She jumped out of bed, grabbed a robe to cover herself, and scurried onto the deck. Abraham was waiting for her.

"No need to rush, m'lady. It was only a warning shot."

"A what?" she said, then looked around. The deck was empty except for herself and Abraham. Eli was standing at the helm, manning the steering wheel. "Where's the crew?"

"Back in Encornet, m'lady," he said, hands up as though

trying to reassure her, "You see, a small ship like The Devil's Grog only needs a crew of two or three if they know what they're doing. The Captain and I have spent more time flying above the land than we have standing on it. We could run this ship ourselves if the need called for it, as it does presently. Go ahead and get yourself dressed, and we'll get out of this quickly."

Another explosion erupted off the portside, followed by a cannonball whizzing past the ship and careening off into the clouds.

"Someone's shooting at us," Verity shouted. As if to confirm her suspicions, she saw a black shape slipping in and out of the clouds to the port side of The Devil's Grog, obviously another airship on an intercept course. She turned her head and saw a similar dark shape on the starboard side as well. Two airships were clearly closing in on The Devil's Grog and were firing cannonballs at her as well.

"Don't worry," shouted Eli from the steering wheel, "they won't hit us. They just want to get our attention and let us know they're here."

"You see, m'lady," said Abraham, attempting to coax her back into the bedchamber as he talked, but still maintaining a polite distance so as not to upset her further, "they won't sink us, as you're on board. Those are gendarmes from the New Continent. If they were to hit us, we might not survive the attack, and they would not only lose arresting a well-known pirate and his crew, such as it is, but they would lose their treasure as well, mainly yourself. They're simply here to escort us to our final destination."

"The New Continent?" asked Verity, as she allowed herself to be ushered back into the bedchamber.

"Of course, m'lady. The Captain said you would be returned to your father's plantation on Bourbonia unharmed, and so you shall. These gentlemen are just here to make sure that happens and to let us know who's in charge once we get there. Not to worry. Now, if you'll excuse me, I have to help the Captain with the ship. It's manageable with a crew of two, but a crew of one will struggle mightily, and that's not advantageous in our current situation. Please, take your time to prepare yourself and let me and the Captain take it from here."

Verity stepped into the bedchamber and collapsed into the armchair, stunned. She could feel a deep emotional pressure in her chest and tried to fight against it, but eventually gave in, putting her head into her hands and crying. Less than a week ago, she was the lady of a manor, daughter of a lord, and living a life of luxury in what amounted to little more than a gilded cage. Since then, she had been kidnapped by airship pirates, had dined with a pirate captain on multiple occasions, had been threatened, had seen an actual duel, had seen a man killed in cold blood, and had spent a night in a brothel in Encornet. She had been relatively unharmed and had, for the first time in her life, been willing to give herself to man fully and of her own volition, and not because her father had negotiated a decent bargaining price or enhanced some trade deal with another family.

And what a man. She could close her eyes and smell Eli's delicious aroma, that heady mix of sweat and citrus and natural musk that only a man's body could create. She could fall asleep now dreaming of the way she felt in his hands as they waltzed, not in a way that the gentry danced, showing themselves off to each other like peacocks, but in the way a simple man attempts to enchant a woman whom he wants to know further. She could imagine the feeling of his body beneath her fingers, the tight muscled figure of a man who worked for a living instead of making deals over brandy and cigars. And while Eli was certainly no stranger to the luxuries and comforts of this world, he was clearly not seduced or corrupted by them the way some men were.

What was worse was that for a few brief days, she had been truly free and happy, all because of this man. At that instant, ugly, salty tears streaming down her cheeks, she knew she had lost her heart to him.

And now he was on his way to deliver her up to her father, who would keep her in some manner as a bargaining chip and probably arrest Eli and Abraham as well for kidnapping her. She chastised herself for asking for such a stupid bargain, and cursed Grotius and all his rules for allowing this to happen. She would gladly give up her dowry and all the livre in the world to spend one more moment with Eli. Instead, she would grow plump in the swelter of Bourbonia until some lord or another wedded her and fattened her with his babies.

Another explosion and its ensuing cannonball rattled the window and shook Verity from her self-condemnation. She could at least be presentable when she was surrendered to her father. She cleaned her face in the washbasin and went to the wardrobe. She fingered the various dresses, deciding which one would be most agreeable for her father. She decided to try on a deep burgundy traveling suit with an equestrian jacket and ruffled collar. It was perhaps a bit casual, but considering the occasion, certainly more than appropriate. She was surprised that it fit quite well as she adjusted herself in the mirror, and realized that she never stopped to consider why Eli had a wardrobe full of women's dresses in his bedchamber and why all of them seemed to fit her, more or less.

There was a knock on the door, and she heard Abraham's voice. "M'lady, are you decent? We're beginning our descent to Bourbonia."

"Indeed, Mr. Screw. You may enter."

Abraham walked into the room. He was normally dressed casually, but never this disheveled. His clothes, always neat and tidy, though worn, had been replaced with what could only be described as rags. Seams were scattered across the outfit, and it seemed the clothes were more patches and holes than original cloth. He was also dirty, almost as though he had dusted himself with coal.

"It's just a bit of theatrics, m'lady. Don't you fret. The gendarme expects pirates, and they'll be thrown off too much if they don't receive pirates. We need to keep them comfortable for a bit while we sort things out. I should warn you that the Captain'll be practicing his thespian talents as well, but it's still him underneath. We take care of our own."

"I would expect no less, Mr. Screw. However, as I'm about to be traded over for what I assume is quite a substantial ransom, I'm not sure that I'm one of your own."

Abraham didn't say anything in return, but simply gestured with a bow and a sweep of his hand, indicating that she should proceed through the antechamber on onto the main deck. Verity straightened her shoulders and struck a pose of defiance and marched out on to the deck.

She almost broke her apathetic façade with a fit of laughter when she saw Eli. Much like Abraham, he had eschewed his regular clothes for an outfit that was much more theatrical and, honestly, ridiculous. Instead of his usual work attire, he was decked in a resplendent crimson army tunic festooned with overly large brass buttons and enough gold braid to drown a man. From the collar to the shoulder boards to the cuffs, everything was decorated with fringe and trim. His black trousers were trimmed with gold piping down the side and tucked into knee high boots that had been polished to a point of absurdity. However, what drew her attention from the ridiculous outfit had to be the hat. It was a suede bicorn decorated with gold braids, brass buttons, and a plume of red feathers. Eli had it tiled at an angle that was certainly less than military precision, almost as though it was being held on his head not by gravity but by confident arrogance alone.

"Should I curtsey, Admiral?" Verity asked with a wry

smile.

Eli ignored her jest and barked orders at Abraham. "Take her out of automode, Screw, and set controls for landing. Be sure to ease her in gentle. This is a plantation landing field, probably offered out to the cheapest bidder, and not some city tower. We wouldn't want to frighten our hosts with our rough and rowdy ways from the start, now would we?"

Abraham saluted smartly and scurried off to the steering wheel. Verity saw the docking guides and flags, which they were quickly approaching, and realized that they were not landing in any coastal city and driving a hansom to her father's plantation. They were actually landing at her father's plantation, and from the look of it, the main field close to the manor itself. Only her father's private ships and those of his closest business partners were allowed to land here.

They eased softly to sandy ground with a mere bump, and Verity heard the hiss of the ship's landing mechanisms shuddering into place.

"Steel yourself, Lady Wheelwright," Eli said softly, almost as a whisper, "this will get ugly before it gets better."

Screw came running back to them and tossed a long, thin bundle to Eli, who caught it deftly with one hand. Screw then stood behind Verity, and whispered, "My deepest apologies, m'lady. Rest assured—it's not loaded."

Before Verity could ask what he meant, the gangway clattered into place and a dozen gendarmes rushed up, rifles at the ready and pointed at them. At almost the same time, Eli snapped his wrist and unfurled a white flag from the pole that Abraham had tossed him. Abraham himself had grabbed Verity by the shoulder and pointed a pistol at her head. All of this happened in a matter of seconds, and Verity felt her body go rigid with terror.

Another gendarme, clearly a superior, marched up behind the others brandishing a sheaf of papers and began shouting.

"Eli Callahan, you are under arrest for the crimes of piracy, kidnapping, wanton destruction, and . . ."

The man never got a chance to finish. Eli walked up to him and jabbed him in the belly with the flag, knocking the breath out of him. "Shut up, you ill-nurtured puttock," Eli said, in an accent that Verity had never heard. "You and the rest of your arrogant, fen-sucked toadstools can get the hell off my ship and go back to sucking each other's cocks like the good little boys you are. I'm carrying the drapeau blanc, you frothy, mildew-eared turds, and that means you can't touch me under the laws of Grotius. I demand to speak with Lord Wheelwright, and him alone, and the rest of you puking, open-assed maggots can crawl back to the whore's cunts from whence you came. Is that clear?"

"You pirate scum," spat the head of the gendarmes, standing upright, "we will arrest you and your crew for piracy, and you will be found guilty and hang from your necks until your heads pop off like a cork. Do you understand?"

Eli shot the man a cold, penetrating look and said, "Lay one finger on me or my crew, and I will be forced to tell Lord Wheelwright that his daughter's head has been splattered across my deck due to your incompetence. Do you understand?"

Verity heard the click of Abraham's pistol being cocked. The tension in the air, and the fear of all the rifles pointed at them, overtook her and began to tremble and weep.

"Stand down, captain, stand down!" shouted a voice. Verity knew that voice. She wiped the tears from her eyes as her father lumbered quickly up the gangway. "I will meet with this rogue and hear his terms. For the love of Christ, man, stand your men down. Can't you see you're frightening my child?"

Lord Wheelwright had always been a round man, but it seemed to Verity that he had gained even more weight since she last saw him. The buttons on his double-breasted waist-coat were almost to the point of bursting, and his chin hung over his cravat like a plump wattle. He adjusted his brushed frock coat with one hand while leaning on his walking stick with the other. Then he reached into his pocket to retrieve a handkerchief, which he used to dab the sweat from his forehead as he stood there panting.

"My Lord Wheelwright," the gendarme captain said, "we have orders."

"Blast your orders, you incompetent fool. You are on my property and I know my rights. I say I will meet with this man and hear his terms, and so I shall. Now get your men away from here and have them stop pointing their rifles at my daughter before she passes out from fright."

The gendarme captain waved his hand reluctantly, and his men began to slink away, still wary and clearly ready to shoot at anything they felt was untoward. Their captain opened his mouth to speak, but Lord Wheelwright interrupted him before he could say anything. "Oh, do shut up. I pay your salary with taxes on my qunubu crop, and I'm not going to have you waving your silly papers around like you own the place." He turned to Eli. "Now, sir, I acknowledge your drapeau blanc and will hear your terms."

Eli doffed his hat and said, "Lord Wheelwright, we ask that you entertain us for forty-eight hours. Within that time, neither myself nor my crew will be harmed nor threatened in any manner. You will provide us room and board befitting men of our station and will make yourself available to me so that we may arrange certain financial and business agreements. After that forty-eight hours, you will allow me and my crew to return to our ship and leave this place unharmed. Our ship will not be accosted nor followed for at least another forty-eight hours after we depart, and you will not instruct the gendarmes nor any other authority to pursue us, nor will you aid them in their pursuit should they request it. In exchange for meeting these conditions, I will return your daughter to you unharmed, unsoiled, and no worse for the journey. Do we have an agreement, sir?"

"Yes, yes, of course," said Lord Wheelwright, hurrying over to where Verity stood. Abraham stepped back and quickly holstered his pistol as Lord Wheelwright took Verity by the shoulder and helped her walk down the gangway. "Oh, my dear, are you quite well? Have you been harmed at all? I was so worried. Please forgive me."

Verity was quite flustered and confused. Normally her father was a shrewd negotiator, and would never give into a bargain so easily, even if it was for her life and safety. This was most uncharacteristic of him. He hurried her down the gangway, and at its end, Verity saw Prudence waiting for her.

"Oh, my lady," she cried, wrapping her arms around Verity and moving her towards the manor, "I'm so glad you're safe. I was so afraid when we left you that something would happen. You were so brave, and I would never have forgiven myself if those ruffians had laid a finger on you." Prudence continued to pet her and dote on her as they walked toward the manor—apparently she didn't notice Verity looking back over her shoulder with longing at The Devil's Grog and its gentleman captain, Cavalier Eli Callahan.

Chapter Seven: A Dinner Discussion

Verity slept most of the day and was only woken when it was time to get dressed for dinner. Prudence and the rest of the staff bustled about her, making sure she was clean and presentable. The somber blue dinner dress that she was tucked into was fine, but Verity found herself missing the wardrobe back on The Devil's Grog and the luxurious fabrics of those dresses. She had never felt revealing or inappropriate in them, but something about the deep humidity of Bourbonia and the tailored but austere, luxury of the manor felt confining to her, and the long sleeves and the lace collar of her dress felt choking and restrictive instead of proper and tasteful.

Prudence talked through most of the preparations, insisting that Verity was so brave for having sacrificed herself, and how lucky she was that the pirates had left her alive and unharmed. She barely paid attention as Verity mumbled her replies and didn't seem to notice how distant and tired Verity's voice was.

Prudence must have chalked it up to shock and exhaustion. She told Verity a good meal would do her well. "I'm sure those nasty airship pirates had nothing worth eating on the filthy ship of theirs. Don't you worry, though. As soon as you see real food made by a real chef, you'll perk right up. Plus, your father is entertaining a guest tonight, so you'll want to look your best."

They tied Verity's hair up in a velvet hair ribbon that matched the dinner dress, and Verity walked downstairs. She heard her father talking with their guest, and the idea of having to entertain two men and their probing questions after such a wild adventure curdled her stomach. She almost ran back to her room to feign a more serious illness, but if she could survive gendarme cannon fire, she could certainly survive this. She set her shoulders, tilted her chin, and marched into the room. Her father rose from the table to greet her, as did his guest.

Eli.

Verity gasped when she saw him standing there. He had abandoned his gaudy military garb and was wearing a striking black dinner suit with a frock coat and bowtie. The low waistcoat hugged his chest tightly and only served to enhance and magnify his physique. His hair was parted and slicked back like a true gentleman, and he was freshly shaved. The slightest hint of his lime balm hung in the air, causing Verity's thighs to tremble.

"Lady Wheelwright," he said with a bow.

"Captain Callahan." She curtsied, then took her place at the table.

"I'm glad we're all here," her father said. "Our cook has promised us a fine feast. I wanted Verity here to understand our arrangements, Captain. I'm a forward-thinking man, I must say, and don't believe the fairer sex should be shunned from talk of business. Clearly, they don't have the heads for it, but at least they'll understand what men have to deal with on a regular basis."

"You are paragon of wisdom," said Eli drolly.

Verity almost choked on her soup, but her father didn't seem to notice. He was busy shoveling the brown slop into his mouth. She poked at the bits of beef in the broth with her spoon and took another small bite. The broth was hearty, but bland, and the carrots and onions had been cooked to a point of flavorlessness. She took a few more spoonfuls, then put her spoon to the side. Eli cocked an eyebrow at her but said nothing.

The soup course was cleared and replaced with a plate of shiny gray rounds that glistened oddly. Lord Wheelwright chuckled. "I told my cook we were having a working man and a rogue with us, and to prepare some fare that you'd be more comfortable with, captain. He assured me his *aspic d'anguille* would fit the bill nicely. I feel like we ought to go shovel some coal after this, don't you?" He laughed again and stuffed a large piece into his mouth.

"Jellied eels," said Eli to Verity, then turned back to Lord Wheelwright. "Just like mother used to make." He took a large bite and swallowed it down with a deep sip of port. Verity took a sampling bite herself, and her tongue almost curled in on itself. The eels were slimy and covered in a gelatinous coating that stuck to her tongue. The hints of nutmeg weren't enough to cover the strong taste, and Verity visibly shuddered.

"My daughter has a delicate constitution, as I'm sure you know, sir. Her palette runs to the finer things in life, and she's not used to such stuff as we men will enjoy."

"I'm sure have done your best, as any father would, considering the circumstances."

"Indeed, good sir, indeed. I hired you, didn't I?"

Verity looked in shock at the two of them and said, "Hired?"

"Of course. You don't think a famous pirate like Eli Callahan would waste his time on a piddly little outpost like New Lutetia on a whim, do you? No. That bastard Chattoway was holding my debts against me, and I had to surrender control of the town and the manor there to him to pay him off. He insisted that you be there waiting for him when he arrived to marry him, so I used you as a bargaining agent to pay off some of the debt."

Verity slapped the table so hard she made the plates jump

slightly. "You sold me to Chattoway to pay off a business debt? No, *part* of a business debt?"

Lord Wheelwright ignored her obvious rage. "Merely a ruse, my dear, merely a ruse. The contract specifically said that you would marry him when he discovered you in the manor waiting for him. If you weren't there, you couldn't marry him, and it would be no fault of my own. I hired Captain Calloway to get you out of there before Chattoway arrived."

Verity turned and looked at Eli, who shrugged. "It was a good arrangement, m'lady."

"Indeed," said Lord Wheelwright. "I've negotiated with the other men of Bourbonia. Captain Calloway is to be made a Lord himself. I've given him a portion of my estate here and set him up with a decent enough home for a man of his station. Certainly, better than that *merde* you landed here in."

"Father," said Verity, still trying to process everything, "language."

"Oh, do be quiet," said Lord Wheelwright, taking another deep sip of wine. "I know you've heard that much and worse on this man's ship. He did a job for me, and I thank him for it. Now, I have my daughter at home with me in Bourbonia. I've taken care of my debts with Chattoway. I have a new neighbor and comrade in arms. And Captain Callahan can stop traipsing around the world in a rust bucket and live the easy life of a gentleman. We all profit in the end."

"You profit, father," said Verity venomously, "as do you, Captain Callahan. But I hardly see how I benefit. I would rather have been Chattoway's . . ." she struggled to keep her compose, but the roiling fury and betrayal inside her got the better of her, "whore! Than to have to suffer through dinner with the two of you. Better yet, you could have sold me to some brothel in Encornet and let me earn my keep that way. At least then I could set my own price instead of having you arrogant men decide it for me. You'll forgive me, but I find the current company too odious for my delicate constitution, and clearly, I wouldn't have a head for the conversation. Good evening, gentlemen. I leave you to your meal." She stood up from the table and stormed out of the dining room before either man could stand.

Verity made it to the stairs and was beginning to ascend to her bedroom when she heard Eli say, "Verity! Please wait!"

She spun around to face him, filled with fury. "Captain Callahan, I am well aware of the type of man my father is. He is an arrogant braggart who values his bank accounts and social status above all else. I have lived with him my entire life and can deal with his callousness. But you, sir, are a liar. You deceived me with your falsehoods and led me to believe you were a different sort of man, a man who lived not for profit but for adventure, a man with loyalty and integrity. Instead, I find you making a fool of me as part of your business deal with my father. You mocked me with your deceit, you have seduced me with your fabrications, and you broke . . ."

She stopped, tears welling up in her eyes. Even now, the rage and perfidiousness spewing forth in every word, she couldn't say it. She couldn't tell Eli how she felt, couldn't admit that she would give up everything—her home in Bourbonia, her life of luxury, her dowry, her dresses and maids and fine meals—to spend a life with him. She wanted to dance with a man who cared more for hard work and adventure than he did a life of lazy idyll. She wanted to give herself to a man who would pamper her with all the luxuries of Encornet but had the honor to let her sleep alone so as not to press his advantage. She wanted to live with a man who cared more for his ship and his crew than any amount of gold. She wanted him, but her lips could not say it.

"Verity," Eli said.

Her heart skipped a beat. She realized that it was the first time she had ever heard his lips speak her name, and the sound of it melted her. Were it not for her passionate indignation against him, she could have melted into his arm immediately.

He continued, "I beg your forgiveness for any and all trespasses that I or my crew have committed against you. Please understand that our deception, that your ignorance of our plans and our arrangement with your father, was necessary. Your ignorance of our plans was imperative lest we be captured by the gendarmes or worse. Secrecy was of the utmost importance, and I beg that you forgive me and my men for deceiving you in this way."

"I will admit that deception was necessary, under the circumstances, Captain. However, you needn't lead me to believe that our relationship was more than pecuniary."

"Verity, I tell you this now. I am a rogue and a scoundrel and have been with women and partaken of their comforts. I am not free of sin nor am I free of lust. But please believe me when I tell you that my intentions towards you were 'pure. I did not mean to affect you nor your heart. I did not mean to lust after you, nor did I mean to give my heart to you. Circumstances as they are, I must confess that I do yearn for you with every fiber of my being, and were it in my power to make you mine, I would partake of you. But I am, as it were, a pirate. Nothing more and nothing less. I will always be a pirate, m'lady, and you deserve more than I have to offer."

Hearing Eli profess his affection to her shattered Verity's heart into pieces. Her passionate rage melted, and she was flooded with a desire to be held by Eli.

"Captain," she whispered, lest her voice give way to her emotions, "would you have me, I am yours."

"M'lady Wheelwright, Verity," Eli said, reaching out to stroke a tear from her face with his thumb, "I would have you if it were in my power. I have been lorded and honored with property, but more than anything else, I am a pirate. There are times that I partake in the wealth of others at the end of saber and pistol, and there are times that I partake of the wealth of others with the nib of a pen. But I cannot offer you a life of comfort. Your father has given me a title and lands, and with it, honorable contracts and trade deals. But there is something to be said for theft and looting. Something to be said for stealing what belongs to other men, wealthy men who can afford to lose, and partaking in the luxuries which such bounty can afford. I am, above all else, a pirate and a thief. Therefore, I would beg your forgiveness, once again, as I steal from you."

Before Verity could say anything, Eli took her head into his hands and pulled her into a deep kiss.

Verity had lived a life of luxury and was accustomed to opulence. She had tasted rare vintage wine from Hellenia and had been at banquets which featured the most luxurious chocolate desserts from Eidgenossenschaft, but she had never tasted anything as sweet as the kiss that Eli pressed against her lips. It was soft and gentle, but still a kiss of pure ache and need, and if she hadn't believed his desire for her before, she did now. She moaned slightly into his mouth as his tongue slipped her lips open, and she wrapped her arms around his neck and let herself liquefy in his embrace.

Almost as soon as it had begun, Eli pulled away and stepped back from her. "Please forgive my impertinence. I could not leave you without partaking."

"Leave?" she asked, horrified at the thought. After that kiss, after the one moment of passion that she had spent over twenty years waiting for, he was going to leave. She stared at him.

"Of course. I made a bargain with your father. Forty-eight hours to negotiate, and then I would depart. Our negotiations have concluded, so I must leave this place. This was sworn under the law of Grotius and must be obeyed."

"But that was just a ruse," she said hurriedly, "for the gendarmes."

"Yes, but ruse or not, a gentleman must keep his word. If he does not, he is merely a charlatan and a worthless corsair. I will sleep here tonight, then board The Devil's Grog in the morning, and take my leave of the New Continent never to return."

"Never to return?" she said, tears welling up in her eyes again. "But your land and your title!"

Eli shrugged. "Mean nothing to me. I'm an airship captain, a man of the air and wind. I have no interest in being tied down to some manor, lording over servants and slaves who grow my qunubu. That's not any life I want."

"Then why did you agree to come get me? Why did you agree to kidnap me for my father and take me on your ship and entertain me in Encornet and . . ." Verity stopped, realizing that she was rambling. Her eyes pleaded with Eli for some explanation, anything that she could cling to that would give her hope.

"I can only imagine what it's like to be trapped, m'lady. I am not a man like your father who thinks a lady should stay put in some house to make babies and tend to her husband. I figured there was treasure to be had in New Lutetia, and kidnapping a beautiful woman and giving her a taste of freedom for a few days seemed like a fun idea."

"Beautiful?" she asked, barely able to hear his explanation over the fear of losing him.

"There were rumors," said Eli with that irresistible smirk of his, "and you, m'lady, surpassed all of them."

"Then why leave?" she practically screamed at him.

"Verity, you are beautiful, and I would give you my heart entirely if it were in my power," Eli said, doffing his hat and shrugging his shoulders in excuse, "But I am, above all else, a captain and a pirate. Even if I could give that life up, and pace anxiously on land loving you, you and I both know your father, for all the lands and titles he's bestowed upon me, would never consent to our union. The thought of being so close to you, seeing you on a regular basis, watching some other man marry you just so he and your father could enjoy a profitable business arrangement, would torture me. I could not suffer through that agony. Therefore, I must leave. I bid you good-night."

He bowed, and Verity began to tremble with powerless fury. She knew she was exhausted, and since they had landed on her father's plantation, it had been one emotional upheaval after another. Never one to hold her tongue, especially under such trying circumstances, she said, "Good night to you too, sir. You have wounded me, cutting me to my very core, and now you scamper off with my heart in your hands but your tail between your legs, just because my father might not like you. Go to hell, you . . . you . . ." Verity stammered, so confused and wound with anxiety that she couldn't think of any insult worthy of her rage. Instead, she spat, "Pirate!"

Her hand shot out like a viper, almost of its own volition, and slapped Eli squarely across the face. The slap was hard and poignant and was strong enough to jerk his head to the side and leave a red mark on his cheek. Eli looked as shocked as Verity felt and simply stood there, rubbing his face with his fingers as she turned and stormed upstairs, away from him forever.

Chapter Eight: Eli's Return

The morning sun had barely broken over the horizon when Eli woke up. He dressed quickly, and crept quickly through the manor, trying not to rouse anyone else from their slumber. He didn't want to disturb the staff or wake Lord Wheelwright, but most importantly, he didn't want to have to face Verity again. His cheek still throbbed where she had slapped him, and his heart already ached over having to leave her. As much as he wanted to stay and take her in his arms again, he knew this would be best. Lord Wheelwright would never allow his daughter to marry a pirate, even a former pirate, and he could not imagine suffering through life loving Verity from afar. It was better for everyone concerned if he left quickly, the sooner the better. He made his way through the manor and out the door to the landing field where The Devil's Grog was docked. He climbed the gangway quickly.

Screw was standing on the deck, almost as though he had been waiting for him.

"Get her ready to launch, Screw. With any luck, we can get out of here before anyone knows we're gone and have a head start on the gendarmes. I know I made a deal with Lord Wheelwright, but that bastard would break any word or vow he made if there was profit in it for him. We need to be gone, and fast. Let's get the lads and see if we can't find a job in Encornet, shall we?"

Screw saluted and ran to lift the gangway and begin the liftoff procedure. While he was working, he said, "I figured you'd be up, sir, so I took the liberty of making breakfast. It's

waiting in your quarters. I can get her up by myself, and we'll
be on our way. Take your time, sir."

"My thanks, Screw," Eli shouted back, "it'll be nice to sleep
in my own bed again."

He stormed across the deck, slamming the door to the antechamber, pausing only to inhale deeply. She was still here.
Not her, exactly, but her smell and the traces of her. He was
sure the dresses he'd ordered would still be in the wardrobe.
Maybe he could have them shipped to her from Encornet, he
mused as he stepped into the bedchamber, then froze.

Verity was standing at the foot of his bed, wearing nothing
but a simple white cotton nightgown. Her wrists had been
bound to one of the bed's corner columns, and she was blind-
folded. "Good morning, Captain," she purred as the door
clicked closed behind Eli.

"M'lady," he said, then stepped forward.

Verity could not see him but heard his boots on the wooden
floor. She could smell his signature lime balm, and her skin
tingled with the thought of him touching her. "I'm sure you
have inquiries, Captain, but allow me to explain. If you will
not stay in Bourbonia, then I have no choice but to be kidnapped by you and spend my days as your private servant.
You are, after all, a pirate, and a man of your word. You ful-
filled your contract with my father, in accordance with the
laws of Grotius, but there was nothing in your arbitration
about not kidnapping me again and holding me for a second
ransom. And, as you and I have made no arbitration, I am unfortunately your prisoner and must consent to your whim."

Eli stepped up behind her and twirled a lock of her hair
around his finger. "My prisoner?" he said. "Who must consent to my whim?"

"Indeed," said Verity in an exaggerated tone. "I do so hope

my captor will not understand that I am a lady and would never willingly consent to his wild and uncouth debaucheries." As if to emphasize her point, she stepped back slightly and wriggled her backside against him.

"Do not tempt me," he said, smacking her butt cheek hard enough to make her yelp. "First things first, we can't have you tied up like this."

Verity gasped as she heard him unsheathe his dagger, then felt the cool of the steel against her wrist before he adjusted it slightly, sawing quickly through the ropes that bound her.

She fell back against him and he wrapped his free arm around her, catching her and pressing her whole body against him. He moaned against her neck as he reached up with his hand and softly kneaded one of her breasts in his fingers. He quickly sheathed his dagger, then clutched her with both arms, massaging her breasts through the thin cotton of her nightgown.

Verity moaned audibly beneath his touch, arching her head back as he began to kiss her neck. She had waited so long for this moment and didn't know whether to rush, experiencing each pleasure as quickly as possible, or to wait and enjoy Eli as long as she possibly could. She reached up with one hand and yanked off her blindfold, then spun to face Eli and kiss him again. He wrapped his arms around her and kissed her hungrily. Verity could feel herself getting wet, every inch of her skin throbbing with desire. Eli's hands travelled the length of her body slowly, teasing her shoulders, working down her sides to trace along the curve of her waist, then lower still, holding on to her full hips to squeeze her closer. He moaned, and whispered in her ear, "I can't keep my hands off you, Verity. I have waited to hold you for so long."

She loved hearing her name in his mouth, loved feeling his hands on her body. But she still couldn't believe this was happening. "Please," she whispered to him, "Go slowly."

"We can stop," Eli said, pausing his kisses to stroke her hair and hold her close. "I would never want to rush you."

"No," Verity demanded, "don't stop. Please, for the love of God, don't stop." She was surprised at her animalistic ferocity, the pent-up longing and desire coming out in one lusty command, and she hoped that she hadn't shocked Eli or changed his attitude towards her.

"I was hoping you would say that." He grinned and kissed her again. His mouth was wet and soft, and his tongue insistent, but gentle. Verity had never been kissed before, and she felt like she could kiss him for hours. She wrapped her arms around his broad shoulders and pulled his body tightly against hers. She could feel the bulge of his erection pressing against her, and it made her even wetter than she already was. Never letting his lips leave hers, she began to tug at his shoulders, gently pulling him towards the bed.

"I'm going to need your help with this," said Verity, indicating her nightgown with her hands. Eli's grin grew even wider, his eyes twinkling with blatant lust as he guided her arms up, as if to gently tug the dress over her head. But instead of lifting it up, he grabbed it quickly by the collar and yanked wide, ripping the fabric in two and casting the pieces aside.

Despite the fact that the dress was such a thin cotton, Verity couldn't help but shiver a little when the air hit her naked skin. She was encouraged by his insistent lust and smiled as Eli ran his hands over her skin again, stroking and teasing. Verity found herself leaning into his touches, sighing, wanting nothing more than to stand there, right then, completely naked with him. She began to tug at Eli's shirt hem, trying to yank the fabric off his body as he buried his face against her breasts, licking her nipples as the scruff of his beard gently scratched their soft skin.

He put a hand to her back and pulled her close as his lips

wrapped around one nipple and began sucking on it, teasing it with his lips and tongue. She gasped and stopped trying to pull his shirt off his body, letting her hands droop as she arched into the quick, wet strokes of his tongue. She reached up and ran her fingers through his soft hair, pulling him closer. The hunger that she felt for him was insatiable now, threatening to immolate her if she didn't do something.

Verity shook herself out of the libidinous fog that was consuming her body and pushed Eli's head back. She grabbed his shirt again, pulled it desperately over his head, and cast it aside. Sitting on the edge of the bed, she reached up and rubbed her hands across the firm expanse of his chest, fingering the nuances of his body — the soft hair, the occasional scar, each crease and curve of muscle. She began kissing his chest, tasting his skin, inhaling deeply to intoxicate herself on his musky citrus scent.

"Oh my god," he moaned, running his hands through her curls, "you are the most beautiful creature I have ever seen."

His words filled Verity with a hedonistic freedom that she had never experienced before. She kissed and licked her way down his body, over his abs and to the very hem of his pants. "Show me," she begged, tugging at his belt, "I want to see all of you." She tugged his pants down to his ankles and gasped. This was the first time she had ever seen a grown man naked, and by the looks of it, she had chosen the right one. Even by the standards of livre rouge, Eli was huge, and being this close to his twitching erection only made it seem larger.

"Oh my," she whispered, wrapping her fingers around the long shaft and sliding them over its velvety skin, "I see you woke up quite early, Captain." It felt so firm and warm. She stroked her hand up the shaft and let her thumb massage the dark purple head. Then, eager to experience all of Eli, she bent over and let her tongue swirl around the head, feeling it jump in her mouth. Eli groaned, running his fingers back through her curls as she slid her lips up and down his cock, tasting every inch of him in her mouth.

"Where did you learn to do that?" he begged as he curled his fingers into her hair and arched his hips towards her.

She pulled back, and grinned. "A lady must educate herself, and there were plenty of instruction materials in the stalls of Cocotte in New Lutetia." She wrapped her lips around him again, rolling her tongue over the engorged head of his cock.

"Stop," he moaned, pulling her head away from him, "you're too damn good at that, and I don't want to finish before we've started." He took Verity by the shoulders and gently pushed her backwards.

Delirious with desire, she let herself give in to his touch and fell back on the mattress with a giggle. Eli took her ankles in his hands and spread her legs wide. She tried to scooch back in the bed to make room for him, but he knelt down and began working his way up her thighs with wet, open kisses. Reaching her pussy, he licked his way along its lips, tickling her sensitive skin.

Then he lowered his head and began tonguing her slit. She moaned as he made direct contact with its lips, causing her body to tense as her already wet pussy grew sopping. Eli reached up with both hands to grab her hips and pull her down on top of his tongue, and Verity could feel her legs start to quiver as she tried to keep them spread for him. Her whole body was on edge as his tongue became more eager, licking at her insistently and sliding deeper into wet heat. Every inch of her flesh tensed and squirmed as he slid his tongue out of her and used it to circle her clit. She wanted to scream, wanted to echo his name off the walls of the bedchamber, but she was gasping for breath as she clawed the sheets on her bed, squeezing them in her fists as if she was trying to hold herself down on the bed.

Eli's mouth shifted slightly, and he enveloped her

throbbing bud between his lips, sucking on it as he let go of her hip with one hand and slid a finger between her pleading lips. He began to slide it in and out of her, vigorously pumping her as his tongue slid back the hood and circled her naked clit. His finger was caught in a breathtaking rhythm now that only accentuated the pleasure that stormed up from that sensitive nub.

Part of her was in so much pleasure, so caught up with heady desire, she almost wanted to stop so she could find some semblance of control over the situation. But her body continued to tremble and tense until she couldn't take it any longer, and she had to stop holding back and simply let go. Her back arched off the bed as the orgasm shocked through her, spasm after spasm of rapture quaking her as she thundered against Eli's finger and tongue. The waves of pleasure continued to thrill every nerve, so that even when he began to slide up quivering torso, kissing her belly and nibbling at her breasts, she convulsed at every touch.

She was trying to catch her breath when Eli kissed her, slipping her lips open with his tongue and wrapping his arms around her body. She responded by wrapping her arms around his broad, muscular shoulders and rearranging herself so her breasts would rub against his sweaty, naked chest, loving the feel of his skin against her tender nipples. They stayed like this for a few minutes, just kissing and feeling the warmth of each other. But this wasn't enough for Verity, for Eli had awoken something inside her, something primal and impassioned. She had no idea who this new woman was, but she was pretty damn sure she liked her a lot better than the old Verity. She let go of Eli and squirmed out from underneath him. Her body still burned for his touch, and she needed to feel him inside her. She rolled over on her hands and knees and shook her ass at him.

"Come on, Eli," she said, eyeing him over her shoulder,

"take me."

He grinned and stood up, allowing her more room on the bed to bend over. She spread her thighs slightly as he stepped forward, and slid his cock against her tight, soaking lips, teasing her as she pushed back, desperate to feel him inside her. He took his time entering her. He was thick and she was very tight, her walls swelling against his girth. Verity lifted her head back with a low, throaty moan as Eli finally slid all the way inside her. She felt him quiver a little as she shifted her hips and lifted her ass, letting his balls smack her clit. Eli held still inside her for a moment, long enough to make Verity tremble, wanting to move, wanting to make him move. Finally Eli grabbed her ass cheeks, spreading them slightly, allowing him to penetrate deeper inside her, and started to thrust.

Verity groaned over and over as he stretched her again and again. Eli took his time, though, pulling almost all the way out of her before driving into her completely. She was thoroughly immersed in her lust for him, fingernails clawing the sheets as he picked up the pace, pounding into her. Her body took over, moving without any thought, thrills of carnal bliss electrifying her nerve endings and racing across her skin. Whoever she had once been was gone, and the new Verity was wanton and primal, and wanted nothing more than to be ravished repeatedly by her pirate. She succumbed to the strength of his thrusts, the grip of his hands on her skin, and with a libidinous scream, let the climax quake through her body, demolishing any sense of timidity or modesty that had ever held her back.

As Verity squeezed his cock with her wetness, milking it with the pulsations of her orgasm, she felt it twitch violently. She practically snarled as she thrust back against him until he completely filled her again. She began rocking back against him, slapping her ass against his body in a demanding way.

"Please, Captain. I want to feel it. I want to feel you."

Verity heard him groan as she felt him tremble inside her, a gush of sticky-slick heat pulsing deep within her body, filling her completely. Moments later, Eli pulled out and collapsed beside her in the bed, breathing hard but smiling. He reached out with one hand to stroke her hair. She rolled to face him and wrapped her arms and legs around him as tightly as her still convulsing limbs would allow. She sighed deeply and contentedly, inhaling scent of sweat and sex that perfumed the air as they drifted of together in a half-conscious, early morning nap.

Verity awoke in a gentle haze to Eli brushing hair out of her face and stroking her cheek. She blushed, remembering what they had just done. She smiled at him sleepily, and tried to turn her head away, but he snuggled closer. "Did I wake you?" he asked. She shook her head, still processing the night before and the morning and trying hard not die of embarrassment. She was sure that, in the light of day, Eli would be terrified of her and her naked body, that he would regret everything and break her heart by leaving again. She pulled the covers closer to her, trying to hide her body from him.

"You know," he said, grinning, "as much as I love sleeping with you, I think I like you awake even more." He bent forward and kissed her softly. "It was wonderful waking up next to you, though." Verity could have melted into the mattress and died right then and there. Eli was so sweet, so kind, so everything right. "However, I'm sure Screw has had enough time by himself and will need my assistance in getting to Encornet."

He stood and started getting dressed, and Verity blushed and looked at the remains of her nightgown. "I'm afraid I have nothing to wear, Captain."

"The wardrobe still has your dresses in it. They should all

fit you, more or less. I got your measurements from your father before the raid in New Lutetia and ordered them all custom to your size. Take your time, and I'll see you on deck."

Verity took her time getting dressed, then stepped out onto the deck. There were no shoes in the wardrobe, and she had been in such a hurry to beat Eli to the ship that morning that she had forgotten to grab any. She made her way gingerly over the wooden planking, doing her best to avoid any splinters. Eli was at the steering wheel of the ship, and Abraham was standing next to him. When Verity got to them, Abraham saluted smartly and spoke. "Good morning, m'lady. It's a pleasure to see you again. I trust you've had a restful morning."

"Most rousing, Abraham," she said with a curtsey.

"Now, m'lady, if you're going to be with us for a while, I'm going to have to ask that you call me Screw, same as the rest. I wouldn't want folks to think I had airs above my station, as it were."

"Mr. Screw," she said, but he cut her off.

"No mister, m'lady. Just Screw."

"Then, Screw," she said with a smirk, "you must call me Verity until another name presents itself. I do believe once my father has heard of my dalliance, he will no longer consider me a lady. May I ask where we're headed?"

"Well, m'lady . . . Verity . . . we've got to pick up the crew back in Encornet, and then we'll find work there. After that, we let the wind and the fates decide."

"Encornet?" Verity mused. "Would they happen to have a chapel in Encornet?"

"That they would. Called the Cathedral of Those Who Have Given Their Lives for the Air. Airship church, as it were, for those of us that live among the clouds."

Eli, who had been concentrating on steering, raised one eyebrow and asked, "Why exactly do we need a chapel?"

"The way I see it," Verity said, grinning, "my father would send gendarmes to hunt down and murder my kidnapper, even if I was kidnapped of my own volition. However, even he would be remiss to murder my husband."

"That is very sound thinking," Eli said, nodding. "What say you, Screw? Feel like being a best man?"

"My honor and pleasure, Captain," said Screw, and added, "and it's about damn time, too."

"I see that everyone has this planned out without my advice, so would the two of you conspirators like to tell me where we'll be going after Encornet? Or should I pretend to be the captain of my own ship and actually find us a job?"

"Well, now that you mention it," Verity said, stroking his arm, "I did have to leave New Lutetia in a hurry. I left a lot of my things at the manor, and I would also like to thank Lord Chattoway for his generous proposal of matrimony, but also show him what my husband is capable of."

Screw rubbed his chin and said, "We did have to leave quite quickly Captain. I'm sure there's a bit of treasure that we left there. We would be remiss if we didn't at least explore the possibility and allow the lady to thank her old friend. We might even have to polish the long arms for the occasion. It sounds like this lord deserves no less than our best treatment."

Eli said nothing. He simply turned the steering wheel slowly, catching a fortuitous breeze that would help the airship along as they sailed forward to untold adventures.

The End

YOU MAY ALSO ENJOY THE FOLLOWING FROM EXTASY BOOKS INC:

Soul Keeper
Viola Grace

Excerpt

Zeyan was pale grey with nausea by the time they landed. Space flight was not kind to her. Beast had tried to attend to her with water and cold compresses, but nothing worked. Being separated from her world was quite traumatic for her.

She heard Fury speaking rapidly into the com but couldn't make out the words. The sense of urgency was unmistakable. When a rapid knocking occurred on the hull of the ship, Beast left her and opened the hatch.

A woman came in and smiled at Zeyan. "I hear you are having a rough time of it. May I touch you?"

Surprised, Zeyan looked up into eyes that were unrelieved black. The woman's smile showed sharp teeth in lips a slightly darker blue than the rest of her face. The smooth contour of her skull gleamed in the lighting of the ship.

"Of course. But why are you going to touch me?"

"I am a contact healer. I will take your illness and you will be able to meet with those who will take you on a tour of the Citadel. Will you allow me to do this?"

Her head was spinning so badly that she nodded quickly. "Please."

When the woman pressed her webbed hands against Zeyan's head, she sighed at the coolness. A moment later, Zeyan felt pressure on her thoughts and the healer slipped into her mind, taking her pain.

As the healer gasped and recoiled, Zeyan jerked her head out of the woman's grip, "Stop, you are making yourself sick." She unbuckled quickly and knelt at the healer's side.

Fury moved and helped the healer to her feet. "Come along you two, this is best taken care of in the fresh air."

Zeyan's head still ached and her skin was too tight, but the healer's pain was far more obvious than hers was. She moved to help the woman as the healer struggled to stay upright.

They moved together and exited the shuttle.

The sunset was just taking hold and there was a peace that ran through the very air.

Three figures in robes approached them and asked Fury, "What happened?"

"The healer made contact with your new student and collapsed." Fury handed her over.

The contact healer tried to smile. "It was more than I expected."

Zeyan was embarrassed. "I am sorry. I have never done anything of that nature before."

One of the robed figures, a male with wavy blond hair and pointed ears, smiled at her, gently taking her arm and leading her toward the doors. "What did you do, my dear?"

"Her touch was looking for pain, so I gave it all to her. I didn't know she wasn't prepared for it, so I took it back, but it was too late." She could feel the blush as they stared at her.

The healer nodded. "It was more than I was braced for, but if you walk around with that all day, you are definitely in the correct place."

Her companion helped her to the interior of the building and Zeyan was left with the Guardsmen and the two other robed figures.

She didn't know what to do, but when she felt a touch on her mind, she straightened and slammed it back at its owner. The woman on the end swayed and blinked rapidly. "That was sudden."

"I am not used to . . . why are you trying to touch my mind?"

The male with the pointed ears smiled. "We are merely trying to determine the nature of your gifts."

She crossed her arms and scowled. "Fine, take me to a dead body and I will show you."

They stopped and she could see a wave of communication through them. The male nodded. "I believe you can wait on a demonstration. How about a tour of the facility and a description of the training you will receive?"

Her head pounded and she looked to the Guardsmen. "Thank you for bringing me here."

Fury nodded. "It was a pleasure. Call Morganti and ask for us if you need anything. Anything at all."

Fury and Beast both gave her hugs in turn. Fury whispered, "I know what it is like to be hated by your own kind. I survived it and so will you."

Zeyan nodded. "I will get past it. It was just a bit of a shock."

Fury looked her in the eye and grinned. "I think you will. Now, go and enjoy your new home. No one here wants to kill you."

She chuckled. It was funny. "Thank you. It is the best news I have had all week."

The Drai shared a communication between them and each touched her shoulder before entering their shuttle.

Zeyan walked into the safety of the building with the Citadel greeting party and she watched her ride slowly disappear into the sky. She was well and truly stuck on Wetura, the home of the first Citadel education centre.

She looked at the traces of thought zipping through the air

around her, marks of telepathic communication written in a language only she could see, and Zeyan sighed. Learning control over her talent would be easy. Living with it would be the awkward part.

The blond male who seemed to have taken her on as a pet project smiled. "Please, Zeyan. Come with me."

"Fine, but what is your name?"

He placed his hand on her arm. "Orenn, Orenn Deliak, telepath and intake coordinator of this branch of the Citadel. None of us can read you, which makes you fascinating from a curiosity standpoint. I believe that you could be an excellent instructor, given a little encouragement."

Zeyan fought her grin at the contact. It was how she had been able to tell psychics from the general population back home. A psychic could not resist touching her. No talent could. They seemed to crave the contact and once they experienced it, they centered themselves.

Their talents settled and their bodies relaxed the moment they touched her. Unfortunately, the untalented were wound up with tension and panic when she was around. It explained her violent departure from her own world, though it didn't take away the sting of the hate that had followed her right up to the shuttle.

One slip. One little slip at her aunt's funeral and her careful years of hiding what she was dissipated in an instant. When her cousin had sobbed onto her shoulder that she would give anything to speak to her mother again, Zeyan had called her aunt's soul.

When Aunt Leerani had walked toward them, her cousin shrieked in panic and the rest of the funeral party ran. That left Zeyan and her aunt conversing quietly in the drizzling rain.

The authorities had arrived two hours later and her weeks of confinement had begun while trials were held without her. The Sector Guard had mitigated her sentence and she agreed to transport. A week passed and now, here she was, in the custody of the Citadel and looking into the eyes of a man who was offering her a future.

"Well, Orenn, I think I could use some water and I would like to check on the healer who tried to take my discomfort. Can we do that?"

He offered her his arm and she took it, nodding to the others in the greeting party. The woman smiled as they passed and patted her arm, probably not even knowing that she was doing it.

Zeyan resigned herself to tenure of being stroked and patted by the talented. As an occupation went, it wasn't too bad a situation. She had food, lodgings and clothing taken care of. Now, she only had to figure out what they wanted her to do for her keep.

About the Author

Minerva Pendleton currently lives in Cleveland, Ohio. She loves reading and writing alternative histories, from steampunk to weird west and everything in between. When she's not poking her computer keyboard, altering historical timelines for salacious purposes, she can be found working at her local library or curled in the shadows of some quiet cocktail lounge, sipping a mixed drink and reading a book.